CLASSIC PULP FICTION

NEW PULP FICTION

DEPARTMENTS

**Issue #33
Fall 2019**

Rich Harvey, *Publisher*
Audrey Parente, *Editor*

Cover
Harry Rosenbaum

ISBN-13: 978-1702544795

Editorial

by AUDREY PARENTE

THE late Charles Boeckman (by the way, he also sometimes spelled his name Beckman) was a true hard-boiled noir pulp fiction author. In his biography, *Pulp Jazz*, Boeckman talks about his life as a jazz horn player. He was out playing a gig when one of his strongest pulp tales, "I'll Make the Arrest," became an episode of *Celebrity Playhouse*. He didn't get to see it the night of the gig — and he didn't have a television, anyway.

He wasn't married at the time "I'll Make the Arrest" (starring Philip Carey and Jan Sterling) aired. But Charles and his wife Patti Boeckman saw it decades later — When Bold Venture Press was readying to publish the biography, publisher Rich Harvey found a 16 mm copy of the *Celebrity Playhouse* episode. Harvey's friend, filmmaker Brendon Faulkner, copied it onto a disc for the Boeckmans.

A gleaming marble star on the South Texas Music Walk of Fame proclaims Boeckman's horn-playing skills, and his writing is still worth reading, so we share his story "Death Speaks Softly" in this issue of *Pulp Adventures*.

■ Private eye Ken Sligo makes his debut in "New Guy on the Block," a new pulp fiction tale by contemporary author Jack Bludis. This story prequels *The Killers Are Coming*, a Bold Venture Press novel by Bludis. Sligo faces upheaval in his firm's early days, but as with all good private eyes,

the money — and the danger — soon follow.

Nice to know modern pulp-fiction-style writers have the same strong pen and ability as the guys from the early half of the last century.

■ *The Tunnel Under the World* by award-winning pulp fiction master Frederik Pohl (now public domain) was published in 1955 in *Galaxy* magazine, long before the movie *Groundhog Day*. In Pohl's story, Guy and Mary Burckhardt repeatedly awaken to a nightmare scenario of their Tylerton home exploding on June 15. Unlike *Groundhog Day's* happy-ending, the unravelling of Pohl's story is neither comical nor jovial in the terrifying finale.

Pohl spans new and old pulp, since he wrote science fiction for 75-plus years. He edited *Galaxy* magazine, won three Hugo Awards, four "Year's Best Novel" awards, three Nebulas a John W. Campbell Memorial Award, and a National Book Award.

Science Fiction Writers of American named him a Damon Knight Memorial Grand Master (1993), he was inducted into the Science Fiction and Fantasy Hall of Fame (1998) and at age 94, in 2010, won the Hugo Award for BEST FAN WRITER in a blog, "The Way the Future Blogs".

Hope you enjoy the stories and the rest of the old and new authors in this quarterly issue of *Pulp Adventures*.   ■

DEATH SPEAKS SOFTLY

By CHARLES BOECKMAN

**Mr. Pleeber knew
people like himself didn't
have dangerous adventures,
so he thought it was all a bad dream
when he woke up to murder!**

HE CAME out of the smothering darkness with a lurch that rolled him out of the chair where they'd propped him. Swaying there on his hands and knees, he looked like a grey little spider hunting for a collar button. His brain felt as if someone had put it into a cocktail shaker going full speed. He was a thin, pale man with a naturally unhappy face that looked even more so at the moment. The grey fog was still clogging his eyes and ears like cotton. Through it, he could hear, distantly, a girl crying. And that puzzled him. He tried to fit a crying girl in this crazy jigsaw pattern of events, but failed.

Torn fragments of memories flitted through his mind and he snatched at them as pictures in a wind. Mostly, all he could remember was the little fat man with the pince-nez glasses on a black ribbon. He'd never before seen them on a ribbon, except in books. They had really looked very funny on the little fat man, but at the moment Henry Pleeber didn't feel like laughing. He was pretty sure the dumpy, bespectacled man had a lot to do with his unhappy condition. Him and the girl and her drunken brother.

A horrified thought assailed him momentarily. Is that what had happened to him? Had he gotten drunk and passed out?

But surely not on just two beers. Unaccustomed to them though he was.

No, the little fat man had something to do with it. The last thing Henry could remember was the man, reaching up with his thumb and forefinger and removing the pince-nez glasses and smiling at him. He'd looked like a fat, leering frog through Henry's blurred vision. It was as if Henry had suddenly been looking through water. He'd heard surf pounding in his ears. Then smothering darkness. As if he'd drowned in it.

The girl was crying again and that bothered him. Why would Miss Seeiigson be crying?

He had been amazed to discover her with an alcoholic brother. In the bank she had seemed so refined, so genteel. Though he supposed it happened in the nicest families.

But he couldn't understand why she was crying so hard now. True, she'd been tense as a tightly stretched wire all evening, and on the verge of tears. But this was a different kind of crying. There were under-tones of deep grief in her sobs.

He decided to go all the way back to early this afternoon. When he left the bank. He would start there and piece this puzzle together, bit by bit, as his mind cleared ….

It hadn't been raining then, though it was beginning to cloud up. At precisely ten minutes to three, he had placed the "Next Window, Please" card in front of the bars of his teller's cage. He locked his cash drawer and walked out of the cubicle that had been his prison for fifteen years.

He was trembling a little.

The heels of his shoes made little clicking taps on the polished marble floor of the lobby of the big bank. He stopped before the personal savings window and drew out his account. The accumulation of fifteen years. Nearly three thousand dollars.

"We'll miss you, Mr. Pleeber," said Miss Seeiigson, the auburn-haired personal savings teller, handing him the cash.

"Thank you." He toyed momentarily with a brash thought. "How about having dinner with me tonight?" was on the tip of his tongue. He pictured her reaction. Her stunned expression would no doubt resemble that of a cat whose whiskers had just been tweaked by a mouse.

His new freedom was building up in him a growing recklessness by the moment. He whistled a bit as he recrossed the lobby. The porter stopped sweeping and stared at him.

"One hundred in tens, nine-hundred in twenty-fives and the rest in fifties," he told the "Traveler's Checks" teller, and winked.

She dropped her pencil.

As he was signing the checks, she said, "The bank won't seem the same without you, Mr. Pleeber."

He smiled. "I dare say."

He wrapped a rubber band around the books of checks, snapped it once and then strolled down to Mr. Brewer's desk.

A yellow, dust-flecked light ray slanting down from a high window touched his thinning brown hair where the scalp shone through. Pleeber was a thin, stooped man with the careworn features of forty or forty-five. He was thirty-three.

As he approached the desk marked vice president, he folded his heavy bifocal glasses into his pocket, sponged his damp palms on his handkerchief and held out his hand.

Brewer clasped it heartily. "The bank will miss you, son," he exclaimed in his most robust voice. "You've done a splendid job. Splendid!"

"Thanks—" Pleeber cleared his throat and said deliberately—"B.J." He picked a cigar out of his breast pocket, shoved it into Brewer's mouth, put on his hat over one eye and sauntered out of the place.

Benjamin J. Brewer, first vice president of the Citizens Bank and-Trust-Company, was startled. His mouth dropped open. The cigar tumbled down his vest. He stared after his departing teller.

IN HIS small, drab one-room apartment, Henry Pleeber took his coat off and carefully hung it in the closet beside his only other suit, a blue serge. He wiped a speck of dust off his hat, placed it neatly on the table. Then with the air of a conspirator, he locked his door, glanced around and unlocked a trunk.

In the trunk was a boy. A small red-haired boy with a mischievous expression. A boy made out of wood.

Pleeber sat on a straight-back chair, placed the boy on a knee, holding him there with his right hand thrust into an opening in the boy's back and said, "Well, Jimmy, we did it! We're free at last!"

The boy twisted his wooden head, winked at him. "So you finally got up enough nerve?" he cackled in a shrill voice.

"Finally."

"And did you snap your fingers under Brewer's nose the way you planned?"

Pleeber coughed. "Well, not quite, Jimmy. Not quite."

He leaned back and looked around the room with an air of complete happiness.

For fifteen years he had lived in this room, a lonely, shy little man. This room and the bank—they had been his world. But there had been dreams. Fabulous dreams no one would have believed possible of quiet little Henry Pleeber. But they had kept him going—the dreams.

It had taken a long time. First, there had been his mother to support. After she died, he had sent his younger brother through college. Then there had been his sister's divorce. He had taken care of her and her child for several years until she found a new husband.

Yes, it had taken a long time. But the nickels he'd saved walking to work and doing without entertainment and luxuries had added up. To almost three thousand dollars!

And he hadn't missed the luxuries and

movies too much. There had been his travel folders and the books about exciting faraway cities. And his books on ventriloquism. He had spent many a winter's night pouring over them. They had almost made him forget about being lonely.

"We'll get off to a fine start, Jimmy!" he exclaimed gleefully, thinking about the three thousand dollars.

He laid the dummy back in the trunk, pushed aside the volumes and correspondence courses on ventriloquism and got out his huge stack of maps and travel folders. He spread them out across the bed. He was trembling; his mouth felt dry. So long, so many years, so many dreams he hadn't dared hope would come true—now he was actually afraid!

He closed his eyes, described a huge circle in the air with his forefinger, stabbed at a map of the United States. "We'll start … here!"

He opened his eyes. California! Fabulous state. He fairly hugged himself with delight. He was glad he'd picked California.

Hollywood. Los Angeles. Yes, that was the place to start. Long sunshiny days. No more grey bank walls to smother him.…

To tell the truth, he was a bit vague as to how one went about becoming a professional ventriloquist. But he didn't suppose it was too hard. He was very capable. He'd studied hard and he was sure of his ability. One walked into a night club or theater and approached the manager, he supposed. Or, perhaps one contacted an agent of some sort.…

He folded the maps away, put on his coat again and went down to buy his bus ticket.

It had started raining by that time. Automobile tires licked the wet asphalt and neon signs flashing on in the twilight reflected from its shiny black surface.

He turned his collar up and walked along whistling a little tune, ignoring the raindrops that splattered over the brim of his hat.

Afterwards, he seemed to remember the grey sedan parked across the street from his place. He hadn't paid any particular attention to it at the time. And it might have been another car of the same model. But it looked just like the one that pulled up beside him two blocks down the street.

The girl in the front seat rolled the window down and waved to him. "Mr. Pleeber!" she called.

He squinted through the rain, blinked. It was Miss Seeiigson from the bank. Her face was a lovely white blur smiling at him through the rain. He stood there awkwardly, getting soaked, smiling back at her, shyly.

She was motioning to him. "Well come on! You're getting wet!"

He crawled into the back of the sedan, stepping in water up to his ankle in the gutter as he did so. The little fat, bald man with the pince-nez glasses was driving. He could remember that. And Miss Seeligson's brother was lolling in the back seat.

"Mr. Pleeber, Mr. Dielmann," she introduced. "And this is my brother, Johnny, Mr. Pleeber," she nodded at the young man in the back seat beside Henry.

"Hi, Pleeber, ol' Pleeber, ol' Pleeber," the young man grinned blearily, waving a limp hand.

"Johnny!" Miss Seeiigson whispered, her lips pale.

Her brother was a nice looking young man, but his face was weak. And he was decidedly drunk.

The suit Miss Seeiigson had worn to the bank had been replaced by a soft navy blue jersey that hugged her slim young curves and fell softly back from the white hollow of her throat, he looked, Henry Pleeber decided conclusively, like an angel.

But it was funny about her eyes. He hadn't thought of them as dark before. They had seemed a kind of azure blue to him, like deep skies. But now they were nearly black. And she kept putting a smile on that got shaky around the corners and slid off and had to be put back again.

"We were just on our way to dinner," she explained. "Won't you join us, Mr. Pleeber? A—you know, a sort of farewell party? Since you're leaving and all?"

"Well...." he hesitated. "If you're sure I won't be in the way, Miss Seeiigson ...."

"Of course not," she protested. "We'll make you our honor guest. And please call me Mary."

Somewhere along the way, they had stopped at a small tavern tor drinks.

Pleeber remembered they'd sat there quite a while. He'd had the two small beers. He remembered he'd excused himself. When he'd returned to the table, they had a fresh beer waiting for him. He'd protested that he'd had enough, but they insisted he drink one more. This one had tasted a bit different. And in a few minutes his vision had become bleary . . . and that was all he could recall up to this moment....

NOW HE propped himself against the wall and squinted several times to clear his vision. They were in a small, bare room, unfurnished except for a couple of chairs and a rickety table. A dim light bulb hung from the ceiling.

Mary Seeiigson was huddled in the ' shadows on the other side of the room.

Her brother Johnny was lying on the floor in a loose heap. Her sobs had become dry and muffled.

Pleeber cleared his throat. Her head came around and she got to her feet and walked over to him, dragging her feet. Her eyes were red and her face was all twisted and not very pretty. Her lipstick was smeared. She pushed her fingers into her hair.

"He's dead, Henry. Johnny's dead." She kind of hiccuped. Like a child who had cried himself dry.

She knelt beside him, covering her face with both hands.

Henry touched her shoulder. "Miss Seeiigson—Mary—what's happened to us? What does this all mean? My head's spinning ... I seem to be having some sort of nightmare."

"Forgive me," she whispered through her hands. "Henry, please forgive me...."

She took her hands away from her face and pushed her hair out of her face. "1 always tried to take care of him," she said dully. "Ever since our parents died. I tried to show him what was right. But he kept getting in with the wrong crowds. ..."

"Your brother Johnny?"

She nodded. "Before, it had never been serious, mall scrapes I could always get him out of. But this was bad. It was big and

They slid over wet clay to where the sedan was parked under dripping oak trees. Dielmann made Henry drive so he could keep the bank teller covered with his gun.

bad, Henry, They might have sent him to prison for life … or worse.…" She started crying again. "It was just going to be a loan, Henry. Really. I would have paid you back, I swear. I just needed a few dollars to get him out of town for a while. I didn't know about Max …. Dielmann. I didn't know about him, Henry—"

"Please, Mary. I don't understand at all. I—"

A key grated in the lock. The small fat man with the funny glasses came in, scraping heavy mud off his shoes. The rain was driving steadily against the shingled roof above them. The little man took his hat off, shaking loose drops from it. He stood under the light and took his glasses out of his vest pocket and pinched them onto his stub of a nose. His blue eyes glittered down at Pleeber and his pink, moist little rabbit mouth smiled.

"Well. Awake, eh?"

Pleeber got to his feet, pushing himself up along the wall. "Look here, Dielmann, what kind of dirty business is this?"

The small man's smile widened. "Well, we're beginning to feel real spunky, aren't we? Fine! Glad there aren't too many after-effects." He took out a small, ugly, foreign-looking automatic. "I may need this now

that you're feeling so manly. I just killed a man with this gun, you know, Pleeber." He nodded toward the crumpled body of Mary's brother. "Johnny was weak and inefficient. He spoiled our beautifully planned warehouse robbery by loosing his head. He got excited and shot the night watchman. So I didn't see any reason for keeping him with us any longer. He got me into this mess," Dielmann said, his voice growing hard and cold, like his eyes. "And one man can travel much further on three thousand dollars than two."

Slowly, the whole pattern took shape. Slowly, it dawned on Henry Pleeber, the part he was playing in it. His mouth got dry and his heart thudded in his ears. I felt as if he were talking through a mouthful of cotton. "It won't do you any good. The money is in traveler's checks. Every cent of it."

"Yes," Dielmann said. He took out the packet of checks he had stolen from Pleeber's coat pocket and laid them on the table under the light. "But I think we can get around that, Mr. Pleeber."

Henry looked at the girl. Her eyes were pleading with him. "When I got home from work this evening, Johnny was in the apartment, Henry. He told me about the mess he was in. I was frantic. I needed at least a thousand dollars to get him out of town. I didn't have a cent. Then I remembered about you drawing out three thousand dollars this afternoon. I told Johnny maybe we could borrow some from you for a few weeks. Dielmann came in. He heard what I'd told Johnny. He'd been in on the warehouse robbery with Johnny. He insisted on going with us." She shook her head, crying, "I didn't mean for it to come out like this!"

"You should have gone to the police!"

"He was my brother. I—I couldn't think, Henry. I was so frightened...."

Dielmann interrupted impatiently. "I haven't time for chatter." He motioned toward a straight-back chair with his gun, looking at the girl. Reluctantly, she sat in it. He took some rope out of his pocket, tied her securely to the chair, gagged her with his handkerchief. "Until I decide definitely what to do with you, my dear," he explained, smiling.

Then he prodded Henry out into the night with the gun. Pleeber saw that they had been in a small, weather-beaten country house. Lightning flashed and thunder rumbled as sheets of rain whipped up under the porch eaves. On the porch roof a loose strip of tin banged dismally.

They slid over wet clay to where the sedan was parked under dripping oak trees. Dielmann made Henry drive so he could keep the bank teller covered with his gun.

"My house," he explained. "Comes in handy now and then. Come on, get started. I'll tell you where to drive."

The slippery-rutted lane sucked like glue at the spinning tires. They slid dangerously near a steep embankment that jutted over a sheer drop of several hundred feet into a gully. Then they were on the highway.

"Bridgeville," Dielmann ordered curtly. It was a small city some forty miles away.

As they drove into the city limits of Bridgeville, Dielmann mused, "Now this is what I'm up against. In my pocket, I have checks of various denominations amounting to three thousand dollars. But, unfortunately, they are traveler's checks In your name, and therefore require your signature in the presence of the person cashing them."

He pinched off his glasses, polished them on his coat lapel and dropped them in a vest pocket.

"So, we are going to make several stops, Henry Pleeber. We will cash a portion of these checks at each place. I will be standing right beside you with my gun in my pocket. And let me remind you that I am a desperate man. I am involved in an armed robbery in which a watchman was shot, and I have just killed a man. I wouldn't hesitate to kill again."

He chuckled and it sent chills down Pleeber's back. It was like death laughing.

They made six stops in all. Taverns, hotels, drug stores. There was nothing Henry could do but cash some of his precious checks at each place until they had all been converted into currency. It made a neat little bundle. Fifteen years, a lonely man's dreams, his only reason for living, tied up in that one neat little package.

He drove back like a lump of wet clay.

Dielmann tossed the bundle of currency in the glove compartment. He pinched his glasses on his nose and sat back, his red lips smiling, his little fat white hand balancing the gun on his knee.

"Now, I have to decide what to do with you and Miss Seeiigson. Then be off. And I think I have a very clever scheme worked out. Yes, a very clever idea ...."

IT HAD nearly stopped raining when they reached the house. Mary was still in the chair. It was evident that she had struggled valiantly. Her wrists were red and bleeding. Her hair had tumbled into her perspiring face.

Dielmann made little clucking sounds as he untied her. "So much wasted effort, my dear. You see, I tied it very tightly."

He faced the girl and Henry Pleeber. He stood under the light bulb and shadows fell across the pudgy mountains and soft valleys of his face.

His glasses glittered as he spoke. "So nice and simple. You see, the police will find all of you dead. They will conclude that you, Henry, were in love with Miss Seeiigson. After all, you worked in the bank. You followed her and her brother out here. Quarreled perhaps. She was leaving you. You shot both her and her brother, then committed suicide. Yes, the gun will be in your hand.

"That will give me time to get away. I can go far on three thousand dollars." His smile widened until it became a fixed thing. His eyes turned glassy.

Beside Pleeber, the girl drew her breath in with a ragged sob. Her hands were two white knots at her side. A cord stood out. in her throat. Her eyes, wide dark splotches,

were fastened on the gun.

Dielmann aimed it carefully at her and squeezed the trigger.

But at that moment, a gust blew the door inward. The breeze riffled Dielmann's thin, sandy hair. Behind him, from the open doorway, a low voice ordered,

"Drop the gun, Dielmann, and raise your hands.

The little man's rosy cheeks turned the color of lemons, and his grin became sickly. Slowly, he lifted both hands and the gun clattered to the floor.

"Get the gun, Pleeber," the voice commanded.

Pleeber ducked, scooped up the gun. Dielmann pivoted slowly and saw—no one.

He didn't pause to figure it out. How he had been tricked. He moved instinctively, like a cornered animal. He ducked and sprinted out to the car.

Henry Pleeber fired blindly. The bullet went wild. He heard Mary scream. He was running as fast as he could, after Dielmann, pulling the trigger. The sedan slewed around in the yard and spun down the lane, slinging mud. Pleeber stood on the porch, emptying his pistol after it. He saw the car whip out of control, pitch up wildly to the edge of the gorge.

When he reached the lip of the embankment, he saw an orange splash of flame beneath him. Frantically, he slid down the steep incline, bushes tearing at his clothes and face. But before he got half way down, the flames reached the gas tank. The whole car exploded into billowing flames that consumed everything in it—and with it, the three thousand dollars in the glove compartment....

Numbly, Pleeber sat beside the unconscious Dielmann while Mary flagged down a car on the highway. Later that night, there were policemen and questions. A thousand questions. He explained several times about how he was a ventriloquist and the voice-throwing gag he'd used to trick Dielmann. He didn't implicate the girl.

THE next morning dawned grey and cheerless. Henry Pleeber lay on his small, hard bed and looked up at the ceiling and thought that it was just another morning, now. Just like another.

He got up and dressed mechanically in the blue serge suit. He'd get down to the bank early. Perhaps Mr. Brewer would give him his old job back.

The bank leered at him like a huge, mocking grey monster, waiting to swallow him for all time. Mr. Brewer was behind his desk.

Pleeber stood on one foot, then the other, a small, defeated man whose shoulders seemed to droop lower than ever, now. The walls of the great building closed around him, smothering him.

Then a sudden quiet calm filled him.

Brewer was looking up at him, waiting. Pleeber leaned forward and snapped his fingers under the vice president's nose and marched out of the building.

For the second time, the mouth of
(Continued on page 114)

Author and musician **Charles Boeckman** (1908-2015) contributed to magazines like *Action-Packed Western*, *Famous Detective*, *Manhunt* and *Guilty*. He led his own jazz band and (in 2009) was awarded a star in the South Texas Music Walk of Fame in Corpus Christi.

FINAL

THE

3 Cents

Baltimore, Tuesday, January 29, 1946

RS' QUARREL ENDS IN DEATH

stion private
seek public's
ifying suspects

E BLANTON

re   Girls."
in   One barker grabbed
you   my sleeve, but I brushed
their   him off. The rest just
ciates   shouted out their pitch.
sually   Some gestured toward
stopped   the glossy photos behind
Branch   the club windows,
orary to   which usually showed
yspapers   women with pasties
month. I   over their breasts and
ome new   long, slit skirts that
ified what   showed the full length
d about the   of a leg. A staggering
went home   redhead stopped in front
long nap.   of me and asked if I
came back to   wanted a good time.
it was nine-   "I'm having a good
e war was over   time," I said, and I
year, but the   walked around her.
as still crowded   I had managed to
lors out of Bain-   catch a wad of gum on
and soldiers out   the sole my shoe, and I
de and Hollibird.   ground it off onto the
of them were   curb in front of the blue-
ring out, and some   mirrored façade at Wan-
ones were in train-   nasea. I glanced at the
to replace the guys   hand-printed sign that
hadn't come home   somebody pasted at the
he   bottom of the wartime
Uncle Sam

New Guy on the Block

by Jack Bludis

Baltimore, 1946

"Bail bonds, tattoos, rubber goods, and hot dogs," said the fancy-lettered sign in the front window of Sammy's Place. Inside was a lot more, including the pervading aroma of hamburgers, fried onions, and the old grease that went along with them.

I had no idea which of Sammy's many enterprises netted him the most cash, but I suspected it was the bail bonds. I had just started as a private investigator, and for the last month, he had been calling me to locate some of his bond skips so that his strong-arm guys could bring them in.

Sammy, short and overweight, leaned back in the swivel chair behind the desk in the rear of his establishment. Even from there he had a good view of the foot traffic on 400 Block of East Baltimore street, with its strip joints, dirty bookstores and penny arcades. He chewed the stub of his cigar, with dark brown spit sloshing around in his mouth. Miraculously, he kept it from dripping down to his Hawaiian shirt.

"Get him out of here!" Sammy yelled passed my ear.

I turned to see a blond-haired drunk in a rumpled suit stumble to the counter. He looked straight up at me, and the short-order cook made a sudden transition to bouncer. He ushered him out the front door, tumbling him to the sidewalk. He came back wiping his hands in his filthy apron as if the drunk had contaminated him.

"This one's murder," Sammy said, regaining my attention. "But you're a smart guy. It's worth a hundred bucks for you to find him."

In 1946, a hundred bucks was a lot of money. It was just short of what I was getting for a full week's advance as a private investigator. Sammy gave me fifty on the other cases. I located all three skips in less than two days, but they were pretty easy, just punk kids who showed up at their mothers' houses.

He gave me a quick thumbnail of the story, and I commented: "I thought it was an unwritten law? If you find a guy in bed with your wife and you kill them—you're in the clear. Right?"

"Not if he tells his people he was gonna catch 'em at it. The 'unwritten law' only counts when it's a surprise."

"Oh." At thirty-one I was learning something new every day, especially after being out of circulation with war in Europe. The only thing I knew for sure was that I had a living to make. Catching wayward husbands and wives and looking for people and things seemed a better way to do it than working at my brother's butcher stall in the Lexington Market.

"Who said he was going to catch them?" I said.

"Ask the cops." He shrugged and told me that Vincent was a partner with Bennie Traveler in a strip joint called the Wannasea. It was pronounced, "Wanna see ya."

"This one sounds a little tough for me. Maybe I'll pass." I didn't think it was a good idea to mixed up with murder.

"If you don't do this one, you can forget anymore work from me. Maybe you can even forget being a private dick — at least in this town."

Owning any business on the Block implied influence with organized crime. I thought about ignoring his threat and taking my chances, but I didn't want to test him. Besides, I had no other jobs going, and I needed the hundred bucks.

"OK," I said. "You got a picture?"

"I knew you was smart." Sammy reached into his top middle drawer and pulled out a glossy photo of some guy in a tux.

"Looks like a singer," I said.

"He was, before the war. Name's Chip Vincent. His face is kind of messed up now, but you'll recognize him. Here's everything I got on him."

Sammy turned over the eight by ten photo, and while he printed out some information with the stub of a pencil, I remembered that the double homicide happened just before my first job with Sammy.

"He doesn't live far from the club," I said, looking at the address. "Is that where he caught the wife?"

"That's it. If you get him by Sunday, I'll give you fifty extra."

"That's only a couple of days."

"If you want the bonus, you'll have him in."

I wanted the bonus.

Night people are easier to catch in the daytime, but you have to talk to their friends and associates first, and that's usually in the evening. I stopped up at the Central Branch of the Pratt Library to check the newspapers for the past month. I picked up some new detail and verified what I remembered about the case. Then I went home and took a long nap.

When I came back to the Block, it was nine-thirty. The war was over almost a year, but the street was still crowded with sailors out of Bainbridge and soldiers out of Meade and Hollibird. Some of them were mustering out, and some new ones were in training to replace the guys who hadn't come home yet.

Bouncers, who doubled as barkers were in front of most of the clubs shouting out their individual and sometimes raunchy versions of "Girls, Girls, Girls."

One barker grabbed my sleeve, but I brushed him off. The rest just shouted out their pitch. Some gestured toward the glossy photos behind the club windows, which usually showed women with pasties over their breasts and long, slit skirts that showed

---

Jack Bludis has published more than 800 stories under many pseudonyms, and a few of them have appeared in *Pulp Adventures*. "New Guy on the Block" features Ken Sligo, the private eye protagonist of *The Killers Are Coming* (Bold Venture Press, 2015) — but this story occurs predates the events of *Killers*.

the full length of a leg. A staggering redhead stopped in front of me and asked if I wanted a good time.

"I'm having a good time," I said, and I walked around her.

I had managed to catch a wad of gum on the sole my shoe, and I ground it off onto the curb in front of the blue-mirrored façade at Wannasea. I glanced at the hand-printed sign that somebody pasted at the bottom of the wartime poster of Uncle Sam pointing.

"Yes, We Want to See You!" it said.

Like most of the clubs on the Block, they had live music—piano, base and drums. On the runway behind the horseshoe bar was a slightly overweight cutie stripping out of something that once upon a time looked like an evening gown.

I slid up on one of the tall stools and ordered a bottle of National Bohemian Beer. There were six other guys at the bar, along with four women, but nobody at the tables. I wasn't there a minute, when a tiny, straw-haired blonde slithered between me and the stool to my right, and rubbed her breasts against my arm.

"Ah'm Charlene, you want some company?" she said. She dragged out the words in the thick accent of West-by-God-Virginia.

"No thanks, I'm looking for an old army buddy, name of Chip Vincent."

"You know Chip?" She was still trying to be casual, but she glanced over at the gray haired bartender when I mentioned the name.

"We were together at the Bulge," I said. The papers said he had been decorated during the European Campaign, and just

about everybody was involved at the Bulge in one way or another, so I took a guess.

"He ain't been around for a while, but maybe I might could keep you happy while you're lookin'."

"Maybe so," I said. "You know him?"

"Sure." The game was to keep me occupied while the bartender made her a drink and put it on my tab. I kept an eye on him, making sure it wasn't the twenty-dollar bottle of champagne he was working on. When the guy put together a phony mixed drink, I figured I'd put it on Sammy's expenses. He might balk, but Charles "Chip" Vincent had skipped on big bail, and Sammy stood to lose a lot of money if somebody didn't track him down.

"How is he?" I said.

She waited until the bartender put up a glass of ginger ale with ice and a cherry. She stirred her drink, while he stepped away. "He's good . . . I guess."

"Is it true what they say?"

She spoke very quietly. "He didn't kill no wife."

"Why do the cops think so?"

"I ain't gonna talk about that." She looked toward the bartender.

"Is that Traveler?"

"Sure is. And if I was to tell him what your askin', you'd be in all kinds of trouble."

"Is that so?"

She took a deep breath. "Now if you was to buy me a bottle of champagne, we might could go into one of them dark corners."

"I don't want to know that bad." I knew she worked for a percentage on the phony champagne, but I had an uneasy feeling about being there.

"OK," she said, but I could tell that she wanted to talk as much as I wanted to listen.

I tasted the Boh from the bottle and looked straight ahead.

"You really one of his old army buddies?"

"Why would I say it if I wasn't?"

"Chip needs help," Charlene said. She held the glass to her lips so Traveler couldn't see her talking.

"Where is he?" I said, feeling like a traitor.

"Don't know," she said.

"You do tricks?"

Her face flushed so red it showed through her makeup. "Uh, no. But . . . uh . . . I date."

"Good. What time do you get off?"

"If I don't get called by the boss. I'm usually on the street by two o'clock and thirty minutes."

"Maybe I'll stop back," I said.

The way I figured it, the management had already made me as no good in one way or another, and the chances of me talking to her again in Wannasea weren't very good. While I was thinking about that, and with me not so much as glancing at him, Traveler put up bottle of Champagne with a glass for the lady.

I peeled off a ten-dollar bill, dropped it to the bar, and started to walk away.

"Hey, pal. You gotta pay for the champagne!"

"There's enough for the drinks and tips for both of you. Put the champagne on the next sucker."

"Hey!" Charlene called, pretending indignation.

When I reached the front door, the barker-bouncer blocked my way. He was half-a-head shorter than me but at least that much wider. If I knew the routine, he was carrying at least a black jack. I was carrying a .38, but neither one of us would use it unless the other showed first.

"Where you goin', pal?"

"You don't want trouble from me," I said, looking straight at him.

"I don't?"

"No."

Somebody behind me caught his attention. Then he said, "OK," and let me slide by him.

I glanced over my shoulder twice as I strolled up the Gayette Burlesque Theater. Lili St. Cyr was making one of her few appearances in Baltimore, and I figured it was a good way to kill time. After a couple preliminary acts, barkers came through the audience selling 8x10 glossies of the star. They were selling "dirty" magazines and "dirty story books" too but they were only risqué. The real dirty stuff was sold nearby from under the counters in the bookstores and magazine stalls. Sammy even sold some of it, especially the nude glossies wrapped in cellophane.

There were a couple of preliminary acts, then Lili St. Cyr did a kind of reverse strip, by getting out of a bathtub and getting dressed. She did it in such a way that it was far more exciting than the strippers who made that final little move of slipping their G-string to their thigh, and going naked below the waist. It was the only time I ever saw Miss St. Cyr, but it was also one of the few strips I actually remember. Even now it's like a picture going through my head.

After the show, I made it a point to stay away from Sammy's. At two a.m., I sat near the window in a different hot dog joint drinking coffee and watching the front door of Wannasea. I saw my own reflection inside the window, but I also saw the blond guy who had been thrown out of Sammy's this morning. He had cleaned up, and he was nursing coffee at the counter.

At about two-twenty Charlene, in a yellow dress and a red cotton coat stepped onto the sidewalk. She looked around, confused for a moment. Then she walked east on Baltimore Street. A half-block later, a guy wearing a sports jacket grabbed her by the arm. Any woman, whether whore, lady, or schoolgirl, was fair game on the Block at that time of the morning.

"Ah don't think so, honey. Not tonight," she said.

"Come on," he said. "Twenty bucks."

"Sweetheart!" I said.

"Hi!" she said, as if the word were all H's, and she beamed a smile at me.

The guy in the jacket looked at me. His eyes were glazed over, but he thought he knew trouble when he saw it. "I didn't know this was your, uh . . ."

"My girl friend, right. I'm here now."

"Oh," the guy said, and he stumbled away.

"You want to go get some breakfast," I said.

"Y'mind if we get a cab?"

Charlene said nothing until the cab stopped at a place just west of downtown that was alleged to be a tavern owned by Babe Ruth's father. The waitress brought us our coffee before Charlene even looked up at me.

"He didn't kill her, you know."

"You told me that."

"They want him dead."

"Who wants him dead?"

"Traveler. If Chip does time up to Greenmount Avenue, Traveler gets it all."

What Charlene called "Greenmount Avenue" was the location of the State Penitentiary and the City Jail, just a few blocks north of where we were.

I nodded and looked down into my black coffee. I recalled the old saying about not looking a gift horse in the mouth, but I also remembered the one about being aware of Greeks bearing gifts.

"Why are you telling me this?" I said.

"'Cause I don't want nothin' to happen to Chip. He's a good guy." Her speech had cute lilt. I'm a sucker for those southern girls, or maybe it's mountain girls. I can hardly tell them apart.

"You in love with him?"

She didn't answer. Then she went back to another subject. "Why you lookin' for him?"

"For his own protection." It was only half a lie, because if what she said was true, he was probably in more danger on the street. "Where is he?"

"You're working for Sammy ain't you?"

Apparently, my expression had given something away, because her eyes widened. "You are a rotten bastard. Do you know that?"

I knew it.

She pushed back from the table and

started for the door.

"Hey," I called, but she kept walking.

I left two dollars and started after her, but by the time I reached the sidewalk the same red, white and blue taxi was pulling away from the curb with her in it.

I knew from my friend Detective Vyto Kastel that there were seven individuals who, in one way or another, had an interest in every business on the block. Either they owned it, were part owner, or accepted a fee from the owner for protection against everyone, including the vice cops. Traveler, who I had heard about in other regards, might be one of them, so I called Vyto at home. Friend that he was, he didn't give me any crap, even at three in the morning.

"He's slime," Vyto said, referring to Traveler, "but he ain't that far up the ladder."

We had been together on the streets of the Central District before the war. He got wounded early and came back to become a detective. I was back six months after V-J Day. By that time all the police jobs were filled, and I was on a waiting list.

"I thought he was a singer?"

"Yeah, he was a good singer too, but one thing led to another and before you know it, he was breaking skulls and working into a partnership with Traveler."

"Skull breakers don't usually get married do they?

"He was still a singer when that happened."

"Is the States Attorney going to push for murder one?"

"Maybe two counts of aggravated manslaughter. He killed them both you know."

"He caught 'em in bed."

"He knew they were going to be there."

"That's what Sammy says . . . What did you find in his house?"

"Not a thing except the bodies, the suspect, and some clothes he didn't wear the night of the murder."

"Papers said you had the gun?"

"He threw it out the window and into the river."

"How'd you know that?"

"Anonymous tip."

"Middle of the night tip? Interesting."

"Somebody walking along on the other side of the water saw him toss it. The bullets are from the same gun. Looks like a GI souvenir. We got everything we needed. The house ain't even a crime scene anymore."

"Was he mixed up in anything?"

"How do you mean?"

"Prostitution? Gambling?"

"You know the Block. Who's not mixed up with one or the other? And now we're getting drugs, but I don't think it's that."

I thanked him and I hung up.

Kastel telling me that Vincent's place was no longer a crime scene was like an invitation to look. The two-story brick row house on Front Street was a few blocks away from the Wannasea. It backed up onto the Jones Falls River, a narrow waterway that was little more than a sluice for garbage.

I was uneasy as I approached the house, but not about what was inside. A vague thought in the back of my head told me there was something else I should be aware of. I reached across the single marble step and knocked on the door. I looked both ways on the street, but all I saw was an old lady sweeping a sidewalk two blocks away. No one answered the third knock, and it was easy to get in. A head breaker should have better locks.

I eased into the living room, which showed a dim blue through the paper window blinds. The dining room and kitchen on the other side of the enclosed stairs glowed almost gold from the back blinds, putting a shine on the linoleum-covered floors.

If he had shot them in bed, the murder scene would be on the second floor. So I climbed the narrow stairs, stepping lightly where I thought the steps would be nailed to the supports. I reached the landing and looked both ways. There was nothing in the tiny front room except a vanity dresser with a large mirror and a chair. A double bed would have made it impossible to move in there. The shades in the long bedroom at the back of the house were up, and everything was bright.

Somebody had taken the sheets from the bed, but there were bullet holes in the mattress, along with two bloodstains about the size of basketballs. The rest of the blood was smeared in streaks. There was a crucifix on the wall over the bed.

Apparently, Chip Vincent had come to the top of the stairs, taken three or four quiet steps, and let them have it up close, blam, blam, blam. How many blams, I didn't know, but I wasn't looking for evidence of murder. The cops already had what

they needed.

I crossed the room and looked out the back windows. Somebody could easily throw a gun into the river from there.

"Who the hell are you?" said someone behind me.

I turned and recognized Vincent from the glossy. He wasn't as pretty as in the photo, and he wasn't as young either. His right cheek had been crushed at one time or another, and he seemed almost sightless in that eye. He was pointing a revolver at me.

"I'm working for Sammy. I've been trying to find you." It was what I planned to say all along, but not under these circumstances.

"That son of a bitch would sell his own grandmother," Vincent said.

I had no doubt about that, but what I said was "Do you want to come in with me?"

"Hell no! You told me who you're working for, but you didn't tell me who you are."

"Oh," I started to reach for my wallet.

"No, no!" He waived the revolver.

From the light coming through the back windows, I saw that he had no shells in the cylinder of his gun, but I kept my hands up as a matter of deceit.

"Name's Ken Sligo. I'm a private investigator, and pretty new at it. I just got back from Europe."

"Ain't that a coincidence. Me too."

"So your wife was one of those bad girls?"

"Yeah, but I didn't kill her or the guy."

"Everybody says so?"

"Everybody says so because I found

them. I called the cops too. And first thing they did was lock me up."

"They found your gun in the river."

"Not my gun."

"So why did you skip?"

"People follow you, and you start to get suspicious, especially after they take a couple of shots at you. That's all I needed to run for cover."

"Look, Vincent. I've got no beef with you. If you didn't kill your wife, that's fine, because it probably means you won't kill me. But I'm getting paid to do a job. So why don't we—"

"That bastard Sammy. He gets me out on bail, then he sets me up."

"You know the rules. You skip, and Sammy comes after you. You can't blame the guy, he put up good money and he don't want to lose it." It was argument for argument's sake, because I had some other ideas that were just about to be verified.

Behind him, someone peeked around the wall from the stairway. It was exactly who I thought it might be, the blond guy who had been thrown from Sammy's yesterday. He was carrying a sawed-off shotgun, and I could see by the angry look that he intended to use it.

"Look out!" I shouted.

The blond guy thought I was warning him, and he looked behind him. I lunged past Vincent and pushed the double-barreled shotgun up and away, and it blasted off, slamming the wall with shot and scattering plaster onto the mattress along with the splintered crucifix.

If Vincent got killed here in front of me, I would be the major witness to the bounty hunter's argument of self-defense,

and I wasn't going to let that happen.

With his empty revolver, Vincent swung his arm in our direction. He could only be going for a kind of self-orchestrated suicide, I thought as I twisted the shotgun in the blond guy's arms and wrestled him to the floor.

"You've been set up," I said.

"No crap!" he said, and the shotgun blasted off again, this time under the bed, with shot pinging at the springs and bouncing all over the linoleum. The blond guy reached under his coat, but when he saw Vincent's revolver point-blank at his nose, he slipped his and away and let his arm slump to the floor.

I went up on my knees and looked up at Vincent. "Let me take you in."

"Get his gun," Vincent said.

I reached inside the blond guy's coat and pulled the automatic from his shoulder holster.

"You're working for Sammy, aren't you?" I said

"You dumb bastard," the blond guy said, but I didn't think so.

"There are no shells in your gun," I said to Vincent, as I rose to my feet.

The blond guy tried to get up, but I put my foot on his chest and aimed the .45 at his face.

"Sammy'll get you for this," he said.

"Sammy might fire me, but he won't get me."

Sammy had been setting me up to be his witness in the death of Chip Vincent from the first time he hired me. That was why he gave me the easy jobs right after Vincent was arrested, and it was why he

(Continued on page 90)

AN OLD FRIEND

By MICHAEL R. HAYFIELDS

In Mexico, they call him Death's Head, the self-proclaimed Messenger of the Underworld, and a Crusader of Justice by eliminating corrupt government officials and outlaws.

The guards, armed with rifles and torches, rushed around the compound and stationed themselves at the main doors and over the fortress walls. More charged out on horses, stopping outside of the main doors. All stood waiting in silence for the slightest movement, the slightest giveaway that the mysterious marauder had returned. There was light chatter from the soldiers who'd gathered around the complex. This went on for just under a minute when they heard the sound of hooves.

Emerging from the darkness, a bright white stallion raced towards the troop. The commander gave the signal to stand quiet, for on the horse was a figure who significantly contrasted with the horse's tone.

"Alvarez." The commander called out to one of his soldiers.

Shots rang out and a muffled cry came from the horse's rider, before slumping and falling off. Two soldiers went ahead to check the inert form by peeling the hood from his face, only to discover that the rider was one of their unit tied up. Three bullets had struck him in the chest.

"Domingo." The first soldier exclaimed.

The second soldier lifted the cloak from his body to inspect a note that had been fastened to his belt, hanging out his pocket. He opened it up to read the words:

Three innocent lives of strangers have been traded for one of your own. Let this be a lesson. Death gives no warning.

The soldiers turned back, and the commander asked for a report.

"This is not the rider." the first soldier declared.

The commander, his brows furrowed, probed for a deeper meaning. "Then where is he?"

"Bait." said the second soldier. "It was a trap."

Then horrid realization afflicted the commander.

"Then he must be inside the compound."

Colonel Gabriel Mureda had expected Death to befall him, and through this expectation he did not fear it. The personal weakness lied in obsession, his brown eyes watched the large brass clock that swung mercilessly, reminding him of the blade that would swing across the necks of those who opposed him. He had no superstitions about that, a man in his power circle was bound to make many enemies, and if he could not hurt them the next best thing would be to humiliate them.

One of his recent campaigns aimed to rebuild the Mexican government and provide services to its people. However, that came with a heavy price as taxes were raised and each remaining citizen — including laborers — had to pay a larger sum, which they could barely afford. He exhausted his best efforts to make them understand or, at least, see his point of view; but the public outrage was strong. The ones brave enough to stand up to his extortionate malpractice joined dissident groups, and many who opposed his actions would meet a swift end.

He placed a bounty on three dissidents of these groups and reveled in the chance of them being captured. Many were scattered, but they could not resist the might of his army forever. Not unless they got help.

Then he gritted his teeth, recalling the memory of the person who openly defied his system, a crusader of justice known as Death's Head who had made recent headlines. If he could challenge him tio a duel or trap him then all his troubles would cease. These musings were followed by horses pulling up, suggesting new information or new captures. He was so concentrated on that he almost didn't hear one of his soldiers enter his main office with the information.

"Colonel Mureda, we have captured three of the leaders. When do you want the execution."

Mureda faced him, his own countenance sharp and refined with age. His words echoed a brutal efficiency.

"Schedule it within the next hour."

"Yes sir." the guard replied.

Looking back towards the clock he could see that one hand marked the hour of five. Shadows danced around the clock and his face, and were illuminated just as a bolt of light from the tinted sky.

Nearly an hour had passed while Mureda had been waiting in his dimly lit office before he got the news from a small group of ten soldiers rushed up to him, frantic and perspiring.

"Sir, the prisoners have escaped."

"Escaped!" the colonel bellowed. "How?"

"We do not know, sir, but one of the soldiers saw a man flee from the barracks."

The colonel paused. "What did this man look like?"

"I do not know sir." the guard replied. "But he was dressed in black."

Black … Then his denouncer had arrived.

"That is not all, colonel." another interposed. "Some of us managed to see his face, it was white, deathly white."

The colonel grinned. "I know this figure, they call him *Cabeza de la muerte*, or Death's Head. He has come for me."

"Is he an agent working for the dissi-

Michael R. Hayfield is an emerging writer from the United Kingdom and avid reader of the pulps including Hammett, Chandler, Howard, Lovecraft, Doc Savage and The Shadow. He regularly writes for the horror, science fiction, crime, and fantasy genres, working on several stories and screenplays in his spare time.

dents?" one guard asked.

"Or perhaps he is a *gringo*?" added another.

Mureda sighed. "I doubt it, but he plans to exact vengeance upon me once that clock reaches six."

The soldiers had looked on with uncertainty before the colonel roused them up to take arms. "Get all the soldiers you can find and made them surround the complex. He had said: "I do not intend to make this an easy victory for our intruder."

Colonel Mureda, sitting at his desk, got up and paced the room. He looked back at the clock and saw that it was seconds away from the approaching hour.

On the hour of six, he had related in a previous note to the colonel, that death would come on swift wings. Wings implying a form of airborne malevolance, an air strike? A poisoned dart or arrow?

The message conveyed a subtlety that showed this was no ordinary vigilante, rather a brazen vigilante who would not think of exacting his vengeance as a coward should. He seemed like the type to let his victim know death would inevitably claim the intended victim, which would in turn put unbridled stress on the victim and cause the accursed to pursue drastic measures. But not him. Having been an active participant in the revolution he knew the odds he had to face, and if it meant being bested by luck or a more qualified challenger then so be it.

Mureda got up to get himself another drink, as his mouth felt dryer than usual. In usual steadfast manner he went to pull some tequila from a tumbler when a slight movement put him on alert. His attacker had arrived.

"Waiting for me?" a smooth voice asked.

Mureda's eyes blew out in surprise, but they soon relaxed. "You!"

"I prefer to keep an appointment." the smooth voice intoned once again.

"You released my prisoners."

He turned around to the window overlooking his desk to see a lanky figure dressed in a black charro suit with a giant sombrero. He perched on top of the ledge like a hawk resting on a tree branch.

"You're finally here to confront me."

The strange man nodded. His face was dull white but on it were etched black markings, markings that represented elaborate drawings of enhanced skeletal features, as seen in the Latin American tradition of *Dia de los Muertos*. He stepped from the ledge and stood closer to Maureda until they were six feet apart.

"I would offer you a drink but I can see you're have no time for it." He sighed., and added, "since you are not human."

"I am more human than you will ever be, Senor Mureda." replied the watchful grim reaper.

"You say that, yet you are dressed like *El Diablo!*"

The figure leered a perpetual smile. "It means I value integrity more than your soldiers do."

"But you wear a mask, a well-known act of cowardice."

"The mask draws attention to your own misdeeds, and you will not be spared in the afterlife, colonel."

The colonel's grin faded into an

expression of hate. "You must think very highly of yourself. You who prides himself to stand in my room as judge jury and executioner."

The black-clad figure shook his head. "I take no pleasure in this, I simply do it to teach you a lesson: That every action, no matter how small, has great consequences. For that reason alone, I am giving you a choice as to how you meet your end."

Out of his suit pocket he whipped a revolver with an ivory handle and reached back to pull out a large sword with a cupped hilt.

In retaliation, Mureda presented a large black handled cutlass out of his own scabbard. "I must tell you." he said. "That I was once a trained swordsman in my youth."

"I'm sure you were." said the laughing corpse.

"So it is a fight to the death!"

As soon as he spoke those words the colonel lunged at the stranger, swinging down. But the skeleton, remaining methodical, parried each strike that he had to offer.

He did not stray from the action himself as his sword movements came with swiftness and added ferocity. His blade curved while Mureda thrusted. Each time their blades clashed a wonderful and absurd flurry of energy radiated from both parties. Both men travelled light on their feet in an attempt to glide away from danger.

Mureda's opponent had one factor which played to his advantage. The masked man, whatever he was called, displayed incredible acrobatic skill in addition to his fighting prowess. A modicum of this was demonstrated when the fighting carried through to the library. Murader swung once, but the mysterious entity performed a backflip which came naturally for him.

The second time Murader swung, the agile figure leapt onto the very top of a ladder attached to a well-crafted bookcase and kicked the ladder away, thus throwing himself back from Murader's relentless attacks.

The colonel's expression possessed a sadistic quality, as he waited for his assailant to come back down to earth and fight on solid ground. His gaze never wavered, the watchful eyes of a lion.

"What are you waiting for?" he said. "Are you not man?"

"What is it, colonel. Don't you appreciate the thrill of the chase?"

These words got the natural reaction from the colonel, and he inched slow and steady to thrust up at his enemy. But before he could do so the lithe figure jumped in reverse to latch onto a chandelier, swinging to the other side of the room and dropping to the floor where he fled back into Mureda's office. Insulted by this cheeky behavior, he sprang toward the door and spun around to see where his opponent hid, but caught no sight of him.

A few moments silence went by until the specter made a deliberate attempt to appear from the shadows and draw attention to himself with a sterling battle cry.

Mureda whirled round, lashing upwards and outwards with each successive strike. The unnamed specter matched the colonel's speed in the art of deflection. Their hands moved in a rich tapestry of combat, bringing themselves close and retreating the next second, swords twisted, turning in each of their grasps. In one instance Mureda managed to twirl the sword out of his opponent's grip. Though cornered and defenseless, the skull-faced intruder dodged a forward thrust by executing another graceful backflip on the table behind. He jumped and rolled on the floor, retrieving his sword and countering the next blow, despite being still on the ground. With swiftness, he countered Mureda, lunged himself back and regained a standing position.

Mureda poked, but now it seemed that his opponent got faster in countering his attacker. The art of the fight was in his blood, the way a trained dancer could perform the rhythmic assault of the flamenco. But try as he might to follow his opponent's moves, they became too quick for him to behold.

On the dawn of this realization, his opponent discovered an opening, for when the volley of attacks momentarily ceased, Mureda swung up high, with both swords touching for a moment. Unfortunately, the death figure took this as a lapse of physical dexterity, ducked underneath and slashed Mureda in the throat.

Blood poured from his neck, as wine is poured from a bottle, and he slumped forward to the ground with only enough strength for him to look on — towards that which bested him. The black figure, his white features illuminated in the small curtain of light that shone through, plucked a rose from inside his shirt pocket and threw it on his dying adversary.

"Another joins the ranks. You will be the next to enter a new life."

As he is walking away the colonel makes a garbled noise, which attracts the attention of the visage of Death, which turns toward the pathetic figure clutching his throat, swimming in his own blood.

Death knelt down close to Mureda's face. He was in no condition to launch a surprise assault. He instead stared, his eyes ablaze.

"Any last rites, you would do best to speak them now."

The colonel made an effort to speak. His life fading fast, though a verbal

(Continued on page 114)

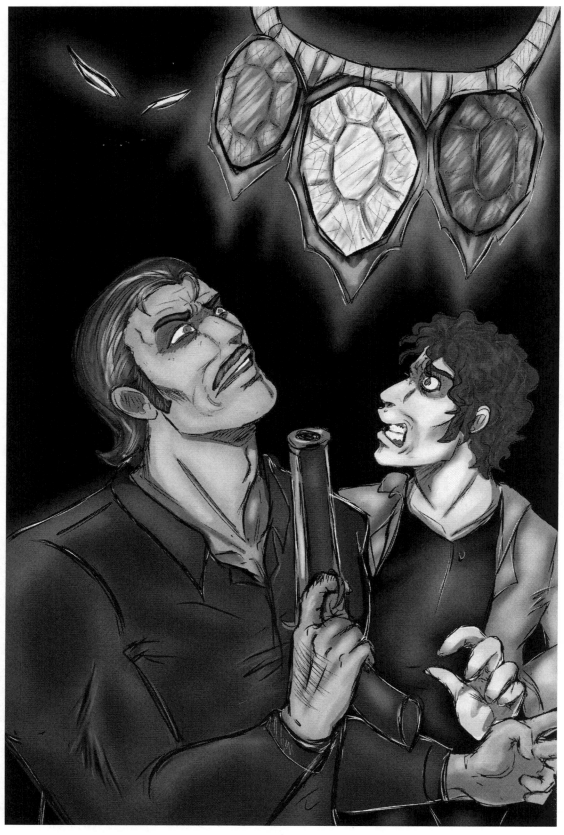

The
Pursuit
of the
Moor

By Teel James Glenn

Prologue

Return of the Rogue

I swear I do not encourage these sorts of adventures. Not much. I am an innocent bystander, in that, I do not set out each day to have my life and sanity put in jeopardy. It just sort of happens more frequently to me than to most people.

In this case I was sitting at a table in an outdoor cafe in the main port town of Kalfia of the small protectorate of Omphan on the Gulf of Aidan. I was having a morning cup of coffee and reading the latest edition of the London Times, specifically an article of mine that the copy editor had butchered horribly, when the commotion at that corner of the town square drew my attention.

There were two of the Caliph's guards, big black fellows in fezzes and uniform shorts, chasing a grey-haired man. They were waving their long truncheons and yelling in Arabic as they ran through stands and stalls in pursuit of their prey.

The fellow the two policemen were chasing was dressed in European clothes and looked almost too frail to be keeping ahead of them. He was thin, grey haired and had a small mustache beneath a long thin Romanesque nose. He dodged and ducked through the chaos he was creating like a much younger man and with the skill of a rugby striker.

The strangest thing about it all was that the fugitive had a wide grin on his face as if it were all a lark.

The trio came lickety-split right at my cafe while all of us patrons gaped. The expression on the harried policemen led me to believe that they were not going to just 'slap the wrist' of the fellow who they were after.

My next action was spur of the moment.

Journalist Horatio Venture meets a legendary jewel thief who enlists the writer in a quest to recover the first and most famous jewel, 'The Moor', from a murderous sultan, but there is a mysterious woman in the mix …

I stood up and quite deliberately tossed my chair into the path of the first of the native bobbies, tripping him. The second constable went head over heels over his fellow with a new symphony of native curses.

The hare to the hounds stopped dead and looked at me. Our eyes locked.

"Good show, my friend," the hare said in a cultured, calm voice, "But I think you've rather put your foot in it." He pointed past me to where three more native police had appeared at a full run at the edge of the square. "I think you had better follow me." He spun and dashed off and I had little choice but to follow.

The hare led me across the square and down a narrow alley, doing quite well at a pace for a fellow who was obviously twenty years my senior.

"Here!" He said. He dodged into a darkened doorway, grabbed my arm and yanked me in, closing the door behind me.

"What is this …" I started.

He held up a finger to his lips. Outside we heard the tramp of booted feet as the police raced past. When they had faded away my host smiled.

"There, done." He said with a gentle laugh. "I must thank you for that little diversion; I don't quite have my old vim." He saw my curious arched eyebrow and added as he extended his hand. "Allow me to introduce myself. Roger St. Simon."

I took his hand and shook it.

"St. Simon, you say?" I asked. "Not … The Moor?"

Again, his laugh that had a swashbuckling quality to it.

"You make one successful job early in your career and you are defined by it forever," he said. "Yes, they do call me that."

I was in the presence of a legend. The greatest burglar in modern history! His first and most famous score was The Moorish Mantle … or simply "The Moor" … that disappeared from a museum in Madrid back in '64. It was where the thief was given the nick name "The Moor." It was a decade before the suave St. Simon and The Moor

Teel James Glenn has been published in dozens of books and anthologies, in many genres, including *Weird Tales, Spinetingler, SciFan, Mad, Black Belt, Fantasy Tales, Pulp Empire, Sherlock Holmes Mystery, SciFan, Crimson Streets, Fantasy World Geographic, Silver Blade Quarterly*. He received the 2012 Pulp Ark Award for Best Author. His website is www.TheUrbanSwashbuckler.com

were connected and though there was no proof the legend grew.

I knew all this because I was a journalist (some had more colorful names for my type of reporting … such as hack and yellow journalist … and who am I to argue with critics?). I had admired the daring rogue … whether it was St. Simon or someone else … for two decades.

But little or nothing had been heard of the cat burglar in the last five years. Now, here I was in a darkened room, out of breath and face to face with a legend.

"I'm Horatio Venture," I said. "I feel a fool that I did not recognize you."

"Venture, Venture," The Moor said. "I should know … ah yes … you write for a number of papers. Did a piece on me about seven years ago, eh what?"

"Guilty!"

He winced comically. "I'd prefer not to hear that word in any context, if you don't mind." He took off his jacket, reversed it to reveal a different pattern and pulled a slouch hat from an inner pocket.

"You did not know it was I when you interceded with the gendarmes?"

"No," I said.

"Why did you help?"

"Seemed like the right thing to do," I said honestly. "Two on one didn't seem very sporting."

"Well done," he said. He listened at the door and looked at his watch.

"I suspect it would be alright to head out and about now," he said. " … but I suggest you change your look a bit."

I took off my own jacket and folded it over my arm. The two of us slipped out of the door and walked calmly down the alley to blend into the afternoon crowd in the marketplace.

"So, tell me, Mister St. Simon," I asked as we sat down at another cafe and I ordered us each cocktails on my company expense account. "What exactly did I save you from?"

Again that piratical laugh. "Myself, I suspect," he said. "I foolishly got caught looking at what I should not have."

"And that was?" I asked.

"Well," he said. He sat back, sipped his drink and smiled. "Let us just say a female was involved." And that is all he would say.

Chapter One
Cherchez la femme

My newsman drive wanted me to press St. Simon hard about exactly what he meant but my instinct told me if I did he would close up entirely to me. So we chatted amiably about nothing in particular for some time till finally …

"Well," he said with that warm smile that had made him such a famous swashbuckler all these years, "I should toddle off. A pleasure to meet a fellow balancer of the scales of justice, Horatio."

Once more a hearty handshake.

"Care to meet for diner later," I asked?

"A midnight snack, perhaps," he answered. "I have the habit of resting in the early evening to make the late nights my purvue."

"Done!" I said.

"I'll meet you at your hotel, The Gabon?"

"Yes," I said. "You surprise me, I'm supposed to be the interrogator."

"You lit your cigarette with a book of matches from that hotel," He said with a laugh. "See you then."

He waved goodbye and almost magically had disappeared into the crowd.

I had one more cocktail then wandered around the town for a bit contemplating what had just happened; was The Moor making a comeback? What grand scheme or caper did this man have in mind? If I could find out and perhaps gain access to his methods and means for an exclusive story, I could make my name in the journalistic circles.

After a bit I returned to The Gabon for a light meal and a bit of an afternoon nap. I had just awoken from that nap and was sitting on the balcony of my suite once more reading the Times and when there was a noise from within the room.

"Hallo?" I called, assuming it was one of the hotel staff had let themselves in. "I'm out here!"

I expected a maid or steward, but the figure that stepped through the curtains from my room took my breath away. It was a woman, but one such as I had never seen.

She was tall and lithe, though with womanly curves beneath an iridescent green dress that trailed along the ground behind her. The dress fairly glowed in the light of the setting sun. Her hair was its own orange flame colored and fell in long tresses around her alabaster shoulders.

It was not her clothing, however that arrested my eyes, but the emerald green of her lambent eyes as she stepped out on the balcony. They were green fire themselves, the orange sunlight dancing in them as she asked, "Mister Venture, I presume?"

Her voice was as lovely as she and I almost made myself dizzy as I shot to my feet to answer. "Yes, but I am afraid you have quite the advantage of me."

"I am called Jada Hessa, Mister Venture." She stepped to beside my table, the sounds of her heels clicking shapely on the marble of the balcony. I stepped back and pulled a chair out from the table and she sat with a liquid grace.

"How may I help you, Miss Hessa?"

"Jada, please," she said in musical tones.

"Then please call me Horatio." I sat across from her and found it almost impossible to take my eyes from hers. "May I get you something? A drink?"

"No thank you, Horatio," she said. Hearing her say my name sent a shiver up my spine out of all proportion. "I have something, uh … important to talk to you about."

"I am at your service." The heady scent of her floral perfume took me far from the human smells of the city.

"It is about Roger."

"Roger?" I admit I should have caught on but I was not thinking clearly in the presence of the exotic woman.

"Roger St. Simon."

"Oh," I said. "What is your interest in him?"

"Interest," she said with an enticing smile. "I like that word for it. Yes, I have an interest in Roger. I have had that interest in him for many, many years."

I took out a cigarette from my gold case and offered one to her. She declined but when I placed the cigarette to my lips held up a lit match, I had not seen her produce.

I puffed and said, "Pray, do tell me what your interest and why you are here?"

"Roger is not well," she said with the musical tone of her voice dropping two octaves and conveying great sadness. "He has only recently emerged from a Turkish prison. Five years behind those horrid, dank walls."

"I did not know," I said. "He … he seemed so healthy and vital today … by Jove, he outdistanced me."

"But he suffered for it tonight." She was quick to add, "He was running on pure excitement today; for you see, he had decided on his next robbery."

"I surmised as much." I lowered my voice to a conspiratorial whisper. "What is it?"

"You must never tell anyone." She said in stern tones. "It could mean his life."

"I am a journalist," I said in all honestly. "It is my job and my duty to report; but I give you my word I will not reveal anything I learn here so as to jeopardize his freedom or well-being."

She considered this for a moment then let out a deep sigh. "I *must* trust you, for Roger trusts you, I know."

She leaned in now. The nearness of her was intoxicating. "Roger is going to break into the Caliph's seraglio tonight to attempt to steal back The Moorish Mantle."

"The Moor itself?" I gasped. It disappeared those many years ago after his rumored theft of it. No word had been heard of it in all that time, adding to its storied history.

"Yes," she said. "That necklace handed down, they say, from the Queen of Sheba herself, a gift from Solomon to her on their wedding day. Now the Caliph has given it to his favorite wife. Roger is determined to steal it. I fear he is not up to it."

"What can I do?" I asked.

"Stop him," she said with desperation in her tone. "Talk him out of it. He respects you, your knowledge."

"Why do you not dissuade him?"

"He … he will not listen to me." She said but there was false tone to the statement; she was hiding something. "What is more, you must not tell him you spoke to me; he must not know I was here. Do not even mention me."

"That is a very large thing to ask," I said. "To talk the greatest buccaneer of this age out of his very greatest feat? Why should I do this?"

"Because it will be his life if you do not; I fear this time they will not just jail him when the catch him … they will kill him." She gave a small sob. "I cannot bear to lose him … again."

There was obviously deep feeling in this remarkable woman for the elder rogue but I was at odds as to just what I could do. "How can I stop a man of his determination?"

"You are a moral man," she said as she rose smoothly and all but glided back toward the door to my suite, a sudden rush of wind through the suite, the only sound. "I trust your morality to guide you."

Then she was gone. It was like the aftermath of a storm or the end of a concert when she left, a silence so complete it was as if she took the air with her. Then the sounds of the busy city preparing for night came flooding back.

I shook myself to clear my mind of her

presence. I tried to find some way to believe I could convince the greatest burglar of the age to give up on his greatest challenge.

And, I tried to convince myself I wanted to. It would be the biggest coup of my career as a reporter to share the details of The Moor's 'comeback,' but here I was suddenly trying to find some way to stop it.

Chapter Two
The Moor the Merrier

I wrestled with that conflicting set of thoughts till it was midnight and I found myself downstairs in the bar as The Moor himself walked in through the door.

He was dressed in a dark tan linen suite with a dark shirt and slouch hat pulled low. He smiled a radiant smile and slid gracefully into the chair across from me as he signaled the native waiter for a drink.

"Good evening, Mister Venture."

"Horatio, please. Good evening to you. Have you eaten?"

"Yes, but please feel free to order; I have unusual habits." I noticed that he had positioned himself to keep a watch on the door and the window.

"I think this liquid meal will do me fine," I said. "I really am here to talk."

"About?"

"Just what were you *caught* looking at earlier today," I said.

He smiled mysteriously. "Something I should not have peeked at."

"It was The Moorish Mantle, wasn't it?" He tried to keep his face from registering surprise, but only partially succeeded.

His drink came and he sipped it with deliberation. "You are very well informed, Mister Venture."

"It is my profession."

"And 'liberating' object de art is mine," he said. "My career began almost thirty years ago with the theft of The Moor." He looked at me with piercing blue eyes. "Have you ever seen it?"

"No. Just engravings."

"Then you have not experienced its power. It is said that the three main gems of the Mantle were presented to the Queen of Sheba herself by the Israelite king, Solomon. She had the mantle made and they say it captured the green fire of her very soul in the emeralds."

His eyes took on a religious glow. "It was looted when the Temple of Jerusalem was destroyed and taken by the Assyrians in 770 BC. It went from king to king to warlord for centuries even on the Iberian Peninsula where it got its name, lost and found again time after time. Finally, the British Museum obtained it when Napoleon was defeated, they say the Little Corporal found it in Egypt. It was such a crime to see The Mantle in that cold, heartless edifice of stone." He got a wistful look in his eyes. "So how could I not rescue it from that isolation and give it the love and care it called out for."

"And that is how your career began?"

"Yes," he said with that wistful smile. "And it is how I will end it; by returning it to the museum, but in hopes they will understand and display it with the love it deserves."

I stared at him with shock. "End your career?"

His swashbuckling facade seemed to fall away. "I'm an old man, Horatio. I did not quite do well on my last 'caper.' Under an assumed name, of course, I spent half a decade in a very unpleasant prison. It took a toll on me; don't feel bad for me, we must all face our mortality. But it made me realize I had to come full circle. A grand gesture, perhaps, but then, I am prone to them."

"Why are you telling me this?" I ordered a second drink, and sipped it as I listened intently, surprised by this revelation.

"Because you are a moral man— you actions to intercede on my behalf when you did not know who I was proves that."

(There was the word again … a moral man … something that my old teachers of journalism would never call me reading the last years of my work in print).

"But why now?"

"The caliph of this protectorate acquired The Moorish Mantle for his favorite wife, a witch of a woman called Yasmina who has decided to have the jewels removed from the mantle and reset. An expert from Holland is going to be here the day after tomorrow to dismount the gems and cut them into smaller forms. I will stop that tomorrow night."

He looked at me with intense eyes again and I saw the spark of the man he had once been, both roguish and challenging at once. "I would like you to serve as representative of the museum and my witness for the world that I shall turn The Moor in to. Tomorrow on the dark of the moon, after midnight, I shall bring it to you just outside the Caliph's seraglio."

There it was, out in the open. I let out a deep breath. This could be an even bigger story than just reporting about a theft. It was almost a Quixoteic story now.

Yet I thought of Jada's words about fearing for St. Simon's life if he went through with the robbery. Then I knew what I had to do.

"I will accept it on behalf of the museum and the world," I said in an almost formal tone, "But only if I am allowed to accompany you on the theft."

It was his turn to gasp. "Surely you jest, sir."

"No. That is my condition."

He considered this for a long moment then nodded with a soft laugh. "So, the adventure begins, old fellow," he said. "I hope you are up to it!"

I hoped I was as well.

I quizzed him for a bit about his plans but he kept saying, "You'll see for yourself," several times till I finally gave up and simply enjoyed conversation with him over several cocktails.

The famed Moor proved to be quite a raconteur, spinning tales of his various adventures, but always with an "if I were this Moor" framing and if he still was sure not to incriminate himself.

I did not get much sleep that night, listening long into the darkness to St. Simon's tales of daring-do while attempting to keep ahead of the alcohol I was drinking and still memorize it all.

Afterward, in my room, I did my best to write it all down in as much detail as I could. It was just shy of dawn when I finished my labors, feeling that, whatever happened, I would at least have a good series of articles, or perhaps even a book, on the career of the astounding and delightful scoundrel.

I just hoped that I was not going to be

(Continued on page 91)

THE CLIENT

San Francisco, 1951

In the eyes of the State of California, Stewart Potts was not guilty of embezzlement, and—given our payment structure—that was a grand thing. After returning to the Sampson & Greer law offices from the courthouse, I led the jubilant group back to the conference room for further celebration. Accompanying me was Stew Potts, basking in his innocence, and my two associates on the case. Awaiting us was my secretary, Joyce Caldwell, smiling next to a few bottles of champagne on ice. A couple of Potts' business partners were also in attendance.

As soon as everyone was in the room and within earshot, I announced, "I'll tell ya, a jury's like an old mutt. They growl at first, but you scratch 'em just right and throw 'em a bone, and they'll be eating out of your hand."

I flashed a grin and signaled Joyce to pop the champagne. Her firm, slender body glided over to the table as short, light brown curls bobbed in her wake. She wore a white blouse tucked into a deep blue pencil skirt that hugged her waist and climbed over her hips. When she reached the champagne, her fingers delicately grasped the cork and she twisted it open like she'd done it a hundred times before.

To the other side of the table Mr. Potts' partners congratulated him. He was a round, balding, fifty-something year old financial advisor that somehow managed to sweat through his suits in San Francisco. I walked over to the three of them as Potts grasped the other man's right hand with both of his, shaking so hard the few stubborn hairs left on his head swayed back and forth.

"A truly just outcome," I overheard as I approached.

I put my hand on his shoulder for a moment, before pulling it away as it came into contact with his dampness.

"I knew Potts was off the hook, until he starting sweating like a pig in heat during cross. Not good optics for the jury," I said playfully, a toothless smile crawling across my face. "Lucky for us they were able to see past his excessive perspiration."

"Here you go," said Joyce, handing out glasses of champagne. "Thanks, dear."

"You know," said Potts' associate, a

by NILS GILBERTSON

"I grabbed him by the water fountain and took him into the trees and that's where they found him, strangled, a day later."

long man with black eyes and a deep widow's peak, "we were worried they were going to take Pottsy down, what with how those prosecutors were talking."

I shrugged. "He had the best voluntary intoxication defense in the book. He didn't possess the required intent to commit embezzlement; the old boy was drunk off his ass. I built my whole case around proving how sauced he was the night in question."

"It's not as if I was trying to steal from my clients, merely some clumsy bookkeeping after a few too many. No need to make a criminal trial of it all. Anyhow, Greer tracked down the evidence necessary to exonerate me, it was fantastic," Potts bragged on my behalf. "A regular sleuth." We clinked our glasses and drank.

After a couple more drinks, I felt a tap on my shoulder. I turned to see Joyce, her face doing its best to conceal consternation.

"Yes, darling?"

"Sir, there is a man here to see you, a large man. He won't tell me his name and he doesn't have an appointment. I asked if he'd like to make one for tomorrow but—but he showed me a copy of your business card and said he'd like to see you now." Her voice trembled as she spoke.

I nodded. "He didn't say what it concerns?"

"No, he won't say a thing to me and, well, he scares me. Something's not right with him."

"It's quite all right, I'll see him." I leaned towards her. "I've had about all the conversation a sane man can have with that blubbering idiot in one afternoon," I said eyeing Potts.

She smiled, her lips peeling apart slowing, her eyelashes fluttering so that for a moment I thought I felt a slight breeze from them.

I took my leave and walked back through the halls to my office. We occupied a floor in a building on Battery a few blocks up from Market. There were twelve of us, small, how I liked it. I started the firm with

Nils Gilbertson is a crime and mystery fiction writer, and practicing attorney. His short stories appear *Mystery Weekly Magazine, Pulp Modern, Close to the Bone,* and *Thriller Magazine*. His Twitter: @NilsGilbertson.

my law school pal Jimmy Sampson a few years back. I was sick of my old firm—stuck in a library doing legal research day and night—and he was sick of the Department of Justice because, hell, it's the Department of Justice.

I turned into my office and was greeted by the broad, hunched back of a man, his stringy, blonde hair peaking out from underneath a tattered cap. He wore frayed Carhartt work pants and a brown jacket. The back of his neck was leathery from years of sun, rain, and dirt.

"Hi there," I greeted, walking up beside him. "Max Greer. Pleased to meet you." I stuck out my hand and gave him a tight grin. He rotated slowly, and looked down at my hand like it had a few extra fingers. Then he glanced up at me. He had dark brown eyes that were shadowed by deep eye sockets. Spider veins crawled up the base of his thick nose. He had patchy, unkempt facial hair. His lips were cracked and weathered and didn't move a bit when he looked at me. He took hold of my hand for a moment and gave it a quick, insecure squeeze.

"This is you?" he asked, handing me my outdated business card.

"Sure is, have a seat." I went around to the other side of my desk, and he sat in the chair across from me, which looked uncomfortably small for his immense frame.

"Now, before you tell me who you are and why you're here, know that if you're seeking legal services, this meeting is confidential. Now, what brings you in, Mr…." My voice trailed of in anticipation of him finishing my sentence. He didn't.

"You're a lawyer, correct?"

"Yes."

"A criminal lawyer?"

"That's right. Anything from white collar to murder."

He looked down at his hands. "And if I tell you why I'm here, you won't go and tell the cops? Is that so?" His voice was deep and firm, yet afraid.

"That's right. If you're here for legal advice, I'm bound by attorney-client privilege and the duty of confidentiality. I can't tell a soul, especially the police. And—I assure you—I take that duty seriously. It's what keeps me in business." I leaned back in my chair. "And while I technically can't advise you on how to get away with future crimes, certain accommodations can usually be made." I noticed a Port of Oakland patch on his brown jacket and figured he was a stevedore who got a little too drunk and beat someone silly over a game of pool.

He nodded, encouraged by my explanation, but not fully convinced. Still, he pulled a couple of big bills out of his jean pockets and placed them on the desk before me. "I'm here because I've committed crimes and I'd like to know the repercussions if I turn myself in to the police."

"Why don't we start with your name, and then you can tell me what's happened and we'll do our best to get it sorted out." After putting the bills in my coat pocket, I picked up a notepad and pen. When I did, he eyed my writing hand menacingly and I put the pen down.

"You've heard of the bodies in Golden Gate Park?"

"Sure, it's all that's been in the papers the last month."

"The first one I found right there in the

park. It was at dusk back in March. There's a playground next to a patch of trees in the southwest corner, near Lincoln Way. It was a boy about twelve. He was alone. I grabbed him by the water fountain and took him into the trees and that's where they found him, strangled, a day later." The tremble in his voice was almost masked by its deepness. He spoke with a subtle eloquence that betrayed his slovenly appearance. He did not look up at me, instead looking down at his large hands, which were holding each other still in his lap.

"The next one," he continued. His voice seemed steadier after getting the first one out of the way. Now he spoke as if reporting the daily lotto numbers. "Was out at Land's End. It was a girl in her twenties on a walk early in the morning. There's a secluded trail out by Mile Rock Beach. I did that one there, but moved the body to Golden Gate Park, near North Lake." He stopped for a moment, reminiscing. "She was tougher than the boy. It took awhile longer. Should I go on?" He peaked up at me; I gave him a cool, expressionless gaze. It wasn't the first time some tough guy rolled into my office spouting off about murders. First thing was to figure whether he's the type of creep who offs young ladies and little boys, or the type of creep who goes around claiming he does just because he read it in the papers. His deep brown eyes sensed my skepticism so he began to think.

"The boy," he said, moments later, "wore a red jacket with gray buttons, he was not harmed besides for the strangulation, and he wore a black ball cap with a red brim. But the cap was not on his body

when they found him. His name was written on the underside of the brim. None of that was in the papers." He paused. "If you need more, check the bedroom closet. Don't forget to check the bedroom closet." The sinister corroboration escaped his lips with a tinge of solemnity.

I nodded, ignoring the contents of his closet for the time being. "Before we move forward, I'm going to need some information from you. Let's start with your name. I have this form…" I looked in my desk for client intake forms but there were none there. "One moment." I dialed Joyce's desk. No answer.

He sat there, wearing an expression like he was making the biggest decision of his life. "Roland Harmon." he murmured. I thanked him and jotted down his name along with 'Port of Oakland longshoreman.'

"I'd like to stop doing what I'm doing, one way or another," he said. "What exactly will happen if I turn myself in to the police?"

"If that's the route you decide to take, they'll put you in a cell on the Rock and you'll never see the light of day again. They'll work you over real good along the way too."

His dour gaze confirmed I gave him the answer he expected.

"Now look," I went on, "I know this isn't a pleasant situation, so here's what we're going to do. I'll get an intake form and you'll fill out your contact information. You don't have to write out the details you told me. Then, we're going to talk about our options. How does that sound?"

His head flinched a bit and I took it as

a yes. I gave him one more grin and told him I'd be right back.

I closed the door behind me, took a deep breath, and thought about going back into the conference room for another few gulps. Joyce wasn't at her desk so I went across the floor to where the paralegals sat.

"Carol, you see Joyce around?"

"Sure Mr. Greer, she's in the ladies room. Can I help you with something?"

"You got any of those client intake forms on you?"

She handed me a stack. I thanked her and went back to my office. When I walked in, he was gone.

That evening I walked home to my apartment in Nob Hill. On the way I stopped at Ben's Bar & Kitchen for something to eat and a drink. Ben's was about the only place I ate and he told me not to sue him when I got a heart attack at fifty. Inside it was dark and smoky and grayer than an early morning walk through the San Francisco fog. In the center of the rectangular room was a smaller, oak square that made up the bar, and surrounding it on the outer walls were wooden booths. I took off my coat and sat at my usual booth and Ben came over to me.

"Max! How'd the trial go?"

"My client's walking the streets a free man tonight."

"No surprise there. What'll it be?"

"How 'bout some pork chops with applesauce, mashed spuds, and green beans. And Old Forester with a cube in it."

"You bet."

"Thanks, Ben."

While I waited for my food, I gulped my drink down quick, ordered another, and smoked a Chesterfield. The man in my office crept into my mind. I thought of his twitching, scabbed lips as he told me the details of the dead boy and woman and invited me to go snooping in his closet.

When I got half a chop in my belly and a few drinks in me I started feeling like a chump. I had no reason to think he wasn't some jokester trying to put one over on me. Probably sent by those damn prosecutors for getting Potts off. He did pay all right though.

I finished my food and drinks, paid Ben, went upstairs and had a nightcap and tried to put it all out of my mind.

The next morning I awoke on the couch. It was where I slept ever since my resolution to stop drinking whiskey in bed. I was greeted by a mild headache and a gnawing sense of dread. I got up, put on some coffee, and fried a couple eggs. It was standard to take a few days off after a trial, so I wasn't going into the office. The lump in my gut told me the next few days had something else in store. The lump was a product of either morbid curiosity or my conscience; I didn't spend much thought on which one.

I checked the papers to make sure no more bodies had turned up in Golden Gate Park. Then I showered, shaved, and put on a gray flannel suit, pressed white shirt, dark blue tie, and hat. Before leaving the apartment I phoned Joyce.

"Joyce, sweetheart, you haven't heard anything from the man who came in yesterday? One Roland Harmon?"

I heard her shudder through the phone. "Nothing from him. A few other calls but nothing urgent."

"Great," I said. "I'll do a little digging around town to decide if I want to take him on as a client. He took off yesterday before I got all his details. His jacket told me he works over at the Port of Oakland so I'll poke around the East Bay."

"Sure. What'd he come to you with?"

"I better leave that question alone for now, dear."

"All right," she said, with both disappointment and relief in her voice.

"I'll ring you if I need anything."

Thick fog lingered over the bridge and clung to the suspension cables as I drove across the Bay. Tall white cranes greeted me from across the water as I emerged from the mist, the sun spilling through my windshield. Colorful shipping containers dotted the Oakland shoreline, Roland Harmon roaming somewhere amongst them.

I parked my Buick out front of the port's main building and went inside. The receptionist was middle-aged woman with a head full of red curls and enough makeup caked on to last her the week. She was filing her nails like her pension depended on it.

She glanced up at me, annoyed by my presence. "You got a meeting, sir?"

"No ma'am, I'm here to locate one of my clients. It's rather important. His name is Roland Harmon."

"Client?"

"Yes, I'm a lawyer."

"A lawyer?"

"Yes."

"Representing the port?"

"No."

"Suing the port?"

"No."

"Representing a longshoreman?"

I rolled my eyes at her. "You writing a book?"

"Looks like you don't have an appointment," she said, eyeing a calendar for a half second.

I leaned on the counter separating us. "Now look, what I have to discuss with my client might decrease the chance of some kind of liability befalling whoever runs this damn port. And, if that comes to fruition, I won't hesitate to tell whomever necessary that you were about as useful as a chocolate teapot in preventing such liability."

She stopped filing her nails.

"And," I continued, "who do you think will make an awful good scapegoat when I tell them all damages were proximately caused by the negligence of a single employee and could have been avoided?"

Now I had her attention. Usually when you throw a few legal terms at someone in a threatening enough tone they start acting right.

"Sir," she said, in a cooperative but stern voice, "who exactly are you looking for?"

"Roland Harmon, he works as a longshoreman."

She called over a security guard, whispered to him, and nodded at me to follow. "He's taking you to the manager on duty. If your man's here, he'll know him."

The guard took me up a flight of stairs and into an office that overlooked the Bay. I looked out across the water at the San

Francisco skyline. It was hiding behind the fog. Behind a desk was a sturdy man with a thick black beard, a cheap cigar dangling from thin lips.

"Buck Preston," he greeted, standing to shake my hand. He wore faded slacks, a wrinkled gingham button down shirt, and a jacket that looked as if it hadn't been pressed since the Civil War.

"Max Greer, sorry to bother you like this. I'm looking for a client of mine, Roland Harmon. It's urgent."

"You Roland's lawyer?"

"Sure am."

He eyed me up and down. "How do I know you're not some debt collector trying to break Roland's kneecaps?"

"I look like a rough customer to you?" I said, wryly.

"I look out for my men," he continued, "I don't sit here giving out their information and whereabouts to strangers all day long. You could be a cop trying to lay a charge on him."

I pulled out my wallet and tossed my California Bar ID across his desk.

"The hell is this?"

"It's a bar card. They only give 'em to lawyers and willing payers with deep pockets on the black market."

"It's mighty nice, but I never seen one before. I have no way to know if it's real."

I stared across the desk at him. He was having a grand old time riding me.

"How about this," he said, exhaling cigar fumes, "if you can prove to me, without leaving this room, that you're a lawyer, I'll tell you all you want to know about Harmon."

He shot a wide grin at me and I returned it with half-mouthed sneer.

Before objecting to his proposition, I eyeballed the room. I landed on a folded newspaper in the trash next to his desk. I got up from my chair, grabbed it, and began flipping through it. Each section that was no use to me I let slide through my fingers, the pages drifting down and littering the office floor. Finally, I reached the financial section. I guess ol' Potts wasn't front-page news. Halfway down the page was a headline: *Leading Financial Advisor Found Not Guilty for Embezzlement*. Below the headline was an efficient story about Potts' innocence, including one of my wonted quotes about 'justice being served' or something of that tenor. Next to the story was a small photo of Potts shaking my hand. Below the photo it stated: *pictured from left to right: Attorney Maxwell Greer and Defendant Stewart Potts*. I placed the page down in front of him.

"Now," I said as he looked over the story, "between the photo, the story, my bar card, and—if you'd like to see it—my driver's license, I've proven my vocation well beyond a reasonable doubt. Time to spill."

After he glanced over the evidence, he looked up at me, took another puff, and then burst out in thunderous laughter. The laugh turned to a wheeze and for a second I thought his bulbous head might pop. Once he recovered, he said, "you lawyers are always real serious types. Can't even tell when a simpleton like me is making a gag."

"Forgive me, port humor seems to have a unique tone."

He hobbled over to a file cabinet and pulled out a tattered folder that had 'Harmon, Roland' scrawled on it. He went back to his desk and looked through it, muttering. "Now tell me, Mr. Greer, what type of lawyer doesn't have his own client's contact information?"

"Your man Harmon took off from my office before I could get it all down."

"Sounds like him. In fact," he said, pushing a few documents over to me, "he's been spotty showing up for work recently. He was supposed to be in yesterday and this morning and didn't show. If you track him down, tell him the boss says he's on thin ice."

I nodded and looked at the second sheet, which included his personal information, street address, and the likes. Parker Street, Berkeley. I noted the height, weight, age, and hair color sections. All matched the man from the office.

"I'm the kind of boss who likes keeping tabs on his guys. Limits my own risk. I take it you're not the kind of lawyer who likes to share what kind of trouble his client's in?"

"That's a good instinct," I replied.

"Even for a price?" he asked, leaning in furtively.

I collected the documents, folded them, and put then in my suit pocket. "Goodbye Mr. Preston, you've been ever so helpful."

He grunted and I got up and left.

I drove north from the port to Berkeley. The address from Harmon's files brought me to a small house a few blocks south of the campus. I parked a little ways down the block and watched the house for about thirty minutes. Then I recalled it was the house of a potential serial killer. I grabbed the flask from my glove compartment and took enough to alleviate the tenseness in my chest. I peered at the house. It was a tiny thing, almost a glorified shed. It was beige with peeling blue trim, and surrounded by a dilapidated wooden fence. I took another quick gulp of lukewarm bourbon and got out of the car.

It was mid-afternoon and the neighborhood was still. When I opened the gate it creaked like it was about to fall off the hinges. I walked up the path to the small porch. The door was open.

I thought over my options. This included forgetting the meeting in the office ever happened and dashing back to San Francisco to celebrate the trial. But, something kept pushing me forward. Maybe it was the notion that there was a killer strangling boys and girls in the park and I was the one person in a position to do something about it. Or maybe it was bourbon and bloodlust. I knocked on the open door. After a minute of silence, interrupted only by birds chirping in the afternoon breeze, I went in.

Through the door was a living room with a couch, a small coffee table, and a few junk-filled moving boxes. I called out but got another earful of silence in return. It was the kind of silence that told you plenty.

I took a right into a short hallway and the smell hit me, my nostrils invaded by an amalgam of chemicals and gaseous rot. I took out a handkerchief, covered my nose to avoid the stench, and made my way into the bedroom at the end of the hall.

On the bed was a large, bloated corpse, the greenish-purple creeping up his otherwise gray face. The sun from the window was beating down on his decaying flesh, speeding up the process. A took another few cautious steps forward to get a better look at the stiff.

It was a large, blonde, middle-aged man, but not the one I was looking for. I noticed a few marks on his throat. Then I saw a wallet on the bedside table. In it was the driver's license of Roland Harmon, which had on it a picture of a more alive version of the man on the bed. I went back out to the living room to escape the smell.

I pulled out a half-empty pack of Chesterfields and thought of the man I met in my office and how he wasn't the corpse in the other room. Either my client set me up to come look for Harmon and find the body, or I had one hell of a coincidence on my hands. I thought over the meetings for clues but it was tough to think. Before I got up to phone the police, the eerie, deep mumble, 'don't forget to check the bedroom closet,' crept into my mind. I got up and went back to the bedroom.

When I reached the closet doors I half-expected him to jump out and add me to his victim list. Instead, in the middle of the closet floor, there was a shoebox and a dirt-covered baseball cap with a red brim sitting atop it. The underside of the brim said, scrawled in child-like handwriting, 'Timmy Rose'. I took the cap and the shoebox back into the living room and closed the closet door behind me. In the shoebox was a typewritten note and a loaded Model 27. The note read:

Sir,

Do not think I am playing games with you. The other day when I ran off, I had an impulse to turn myself in and came to you in good faith. I realized in your office I could not stand the scrutiny of the authorities and ruled out the option. It is not the punishment I fear. It is the eyes on me, the eyes of the masses, judging.

Mother always told me to have a backup plan. If this letter makes any sense to you, then I have decided that course for us. Harmon was dirt and I am less remorseful for him than the others. But now, this needs to stop. If I kill another, please use the pistol to end it. I would do it myself but suicide doesn't agree with my constitution. You can find me in the past each night at sundown. No authorities.

Your Client

I sat on the couch and thought over my next move. When the miasma of death wafted into the living room of the small house, I decided to call the police. Before I did, I brought the shoebox, its contents, and the baseball cap out and put them in the trunk of my car.

When a couple of Berkeley's finest arrived, I told them that Roland Harmon was a client of mine, and that when I came to his home for a meeting, I found him decomposing. I told them they could call Mr. Preston at the docks for corroboration. I left out the whole bit about never seeing him before, the mysterious man in my

Dusk turned to night as I hustled through the crisp breeze towards Lloyd Lake. The moon was a sliver short of full and radiated through the evening mist ..."

office, and the heater and note in the shoebox. I deemed it confidential. I gave them my card and told them who I was and they exchanged glances like they knew it was a waste of breath asking me any more questions. They knew I wouldn't say anything about Harmon or go down to the station without a charge. I gave them my statement and they told me they'd be in touch if they needed anything else, like good boys.

Dusk smothered the Bay as I drove back over the bridge. My flask was empty by the Yerba Buena Tunnel. It was days like this I wished the liver was like any old muscle and grew stronger under stress. I turned off Mr. Keen and thought of how I still couldn't be sure the man in my office was the killer dumping people in Golden Gate Park.

Sure, he knocked off Harmon, but that was a different m.o. He knew Harmon and the two had a beef. Also, the baseball cap didn't tell me much without corroboration from the police that it revealed knowledge of the murder not available to the public. Good thing I had an in. Joyce's brother was on the SFPD and a real talker. In fact, I had a little financial arrangement with him that ensured information only came

to me, and not the other way around. I'd give him a ring and see what I could get out of him.

Then I thought about the note. The guy was no dummy. In my meeting with him, he laid out the clue to look in the closet, gave me Harmon's name, and suspected I'd pick up on the jacket. All this suggested he killed Harmon first and left the note in case he got cold feet and decided not to turn himself in. That's what put his little game into motion. Like the note said, I'd been ensnared in his backup plan. He was playing me, and I was playing along.

When I got back to my place I was tired and didn't feel like eating so I went upstairs. I picked up the phone and rang Joyce at home. "It's Max…yes it's been quite the day. Listen, I need to meet with Phillip tomorrow, preferably the morning…no, not at the office, make it for coffee at Ben's at nine…Yes. Then after I'd like you to come over to help me make sense of things. Thanks Joyce."

I lay down on my couch and was asleep a few minutes later with my suit still on.

"Black coffee, Ben. Irish it a pinch. And some toast. Dry."

At nine-thirty Phillip came in. He was

a wiry man with a twitchy disposition and a mouthful of teeth that were running away from each other. Didn't take more than a glance to guess which sibling came up empty in the genetic lottery.

"Hi Max," he said, joining me in the booth.

"Hi Phillip, thanks for meeting me. I know you boys are busy these days."

He ordered a coffee and shrugged. "A few more dead bodies than usual, if that's what you're gettin' at."

I nodded. "Look Phil, something a little queer happened the other day in my office. I'm sure it's nothing, but it's been keeping me up at night. And I can't have that."

"Sure, what can I do?"

"A man came in spouting off about crimes he claims he committed. Serious crimes. Now, I have him pegged for a nut looking for attention. I was hoping there's a thing or two you could tell me to confirm that."

He nodded and grinned, showing off a few wayward incisors. "The killer, you mean. And you want to make sure it's not actually him." He leaned back, sipping his coffee. "Since when did Max Greer catch a bad case of a conscience?"

I scoffed. "Conscience? You misunderstand. I'll only be kicking him to the curb if he's not the killer."

"The best defense for the worst of 'em, that's how you lawyers think. Well, what did this guy tell you?"

I shook my head. "That's not how this works, Phil."

"Sure, just color me curious."

"Let's hear what you know. Leads, suspects, circumstances surrounding the murders."

He lit a cigarette and started to squawk. "Truth is the whole department is in the dark. We got our top investigators on it and they got nothin'. The guy doesn't have a type. The only common theme is the park, and the strangling. Man, then boy, then woman. He doesn't discriminate."

"It is San Francisco, after all." I quipped.

He chuckled. "It makes him hard to profile. The first was a suit, smaller guy, walking home. Second was a kid."

"Let's hear about the kid."

"Boy, age eleven, Timothy Rose. Was playing in the park and his Ma lost him. She called it in later that night and next morning we find him strangled in a patch of trees."

"In Golden Gate Park?"

"Yeah, down in the southwest corner."

"Keep going."

Phillip shrugged. "I don't know what to tell you, boy was in a red coat, his Ma said he had a hat with his name on it but it never turned up."

"How 'bout the girl?"

"Young, around twenty. We suspect the body was moved. Look Max, we're not even sure if all three were the same guy at this point. Worst part is," he leaned in real close, "we found another cold one in the park this morning. Nothing's been confirmed yet but I'd bet my mother's glass eye it's him."

I thought for a moment and sipped my coffee. "New body, huh?"

"Yeah."

"But, you can say with one hundred percent certainty the killer didn't do anything weird to the bodies? Didn't take any fingers or toes?"

"I can say for sure he didn't."

I forced a grin best I could. "Well, that about settles it. Thanks for the peace of mind."

"Not your guy?"

"Nope, not a chance. He went on about hacking up the bodies after. Hell, I should've known he was a joker; he didn't even get the details in the paper right. Call it the stress after a long trial."

Phillip seemed relieved to hear this. He'd been good at keeping his mouth shut in the past, but this case was different. I didn't gamble with people's ethics. I paid for his coffee and thanked him again and went upstairs and phoned Joyce and asked her to come over.

Joyce took a seat in the living room, her eyes telling me she knew I was in deep with something. I spelled it all out for her. The man in the office, the confession, the port, the real Roland Harmon rotting in bed, the note, the gun, Phillip's corroborating evidence. It was eerie spilling it to her. It convinced me—maybe for the first time—it was real. Then I brought her the note and watched her read it over, her face contorting from fear, to disgust, to consternation, and, finally, to contemplation.

"Oh Max, I knew there was something wrong with that man—that awful man—from the moment I was in the room with him. What are we going to do?"

"That's what you're here for, ideas. I'm fresh out of 'em. I was hoping you had an alternative to filling him full of holes. That is—if I knew where to find him."

I leaned over her slender shoulder, her hair rustling with each heavy breath I took. "That line," I said, pointing to the bottom of the note in her hands, "you can find me in the past each day at sundown," I read aloud. "What is he, a killer or a poet?" I stood back up and started pacing the room.

"In the past," she breathed, thinking hard. "You said the bodies were all found in the Golden Gate Park?"

"That's right."

Her brow furrowed and her tongue wetted her deep red lips as she thought. "Well," she said, "what about the Portals of the Past? You know, the columns by Lloyd Lake?"

I stared at her for a long moment as I thought it over. Long enough for her to mutter, "Oh, never mind."

Then I sprung to the front of the chair, lifted her to her feet, and kissed her on the mouth. "Oh baby," I said, as she peered up at me, dumbfounded, her lashes batting, "what I'd do without you—hell—I never want to find out." I took the note and put it in my suit pocket and grabbed the pistol and put it in my overcoat. Then I dashed towards the door.

"Wait!" She hollered. "What are you going to do? Isn't it dangerous?"

I turned around and looked into her emerald green eyes—eyes that were begging me to stay—and grinned. "Just going to talk to a client, dear."

I parked north of the park on Fulton. I sat there watching the sun descend, dimming the city. I pulled the pistol from my overcoat and examined it, making sure it'd shoot straight. Then I went into the glove. The flask was still empty. I felt almost like doing something heroic, and the flask would've helped. Instead, I took a cocktail napkin and pen from my coat, and scrawled: *Max Greer's last will & testament. Sampson & Greer partnership interest to James Sampson. Apartment, bank account, and everything else to Joyce Caldwell. Except, Buick to Phillip Caldwell.* I figured that ought to keep his lips sealed even if I croaked. I signed it and looked it over. Nothing that would make my trusts and estates professor proud but it'd get the job done.

Dusk turned to night as I hustled through the crisp breeze towards Lloyd Lake. The moon was a sliver short of full and radiated through the evening mist, the invisible droplets cooling my face. I reached the lake on the opposite side of the Portals of the Past—the small set of columns that had withstood the Earthquake in '06. No one was there. The quiet of the setting prompted a temporary peace. As I watched the lake shimmer in the moonlight and the trees sway gently in the distance, I thought it wouldn't be a bad place to die.

Then, a shadow emerged from the woods, through the middle of the columns. It hovered at the edge of the monument, its stillness beckoning me.

I circled the small lake and stopped about fifteen feet short of the man. From there I saw him. He turned towards me, but didn't come closer. His smile seeped through the dimness.

"I knew when you and I met we'd get on fine."

"Why's that?" I asked.

"You have a strong code of ethics."

"You and me both, I guess."

He chuckled. "You joke, but it's true. Ethics is a matter of being faithful to what you are, and becoming who you are destined to be. Ethics must sprout from within."

"That's not how the DA sees it. Now look, I've spent a few good days chasing you around the Bay, so you're going to shut up and listen to me for a second. You have two options. One, we go down to the police station and turn you in. I have a history of getting good deals and that's exactly what I'll do for you. Two, we take you home and I'll represent you for the crimes you've committed if you get caught, on the condition that there'll be no more."

It was hard to see the details on his face in the dark but I knew he wasn't going for it. As he stood there, not uttering a word, my right hand slipped into my overcoat pocket. He took a menacing step towards me.

"They found the latest body?"

"Sure did. You had to go and do another one."

He nodded. "With all of this savagery I've finally become what I've always known myself to be. I do it for the same reason birds fly and lions hunt." He paused. "I'm sorry for the goose chase I sent you on. But, it seems to have served its purpose."

"And what purpose is that?"

"Simple, I needed someone to stop me, someone who I have at least a shred of respect for. I read about you and recognized you as a man of the pursuit. I couldn't ask you outright, you needed to be strung along.

(Continued on page 125)

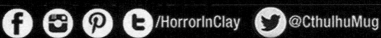

The White Ship

By H.P. LOVECRAFT

I am Basil Elton, keeper of the North Point light that my father and grandfather kept before me. Far from the shore stands the grey lighthouse, above sunken slimy rocks that are seen when the tide is low, but unseen when the tide is high. Past that beacon for a century have swept the majestic barques of the seven seas. In the days of my grandfather there were many; in the days of my father not so many; and now there are so few that I sometimes feel strangely alone, as though I were the last man on our planet.

From far shores came those white-sailed argosies of old; from far Eastern shores where warm suns shine and sweet odours linger about strange gardens and gay temples. The old captains of the sea came often to my grandfather and told him of these things, which in turn he told to my father, and my father told to me in the long autumn evenings when the wind howled eerily from the East. And I have read more of these things, and of many things besides, in the books men gave me when I was young and filled with wonder.

But more wonderful than the lore of old men and the lore of books is the secret lore of ocean. Blue, green, grey, white or black; smooth, ruffled, or mountainous; that ocean is not silent. All my days have I watched it and listened to it, and I know it well. At first it told to me only the plain little tales of calm beaches and near ports, but with the years it grew more friendly and spoke of other things; of things more strange and more distant in space and in time. Sometimes at twilight the grey vapours of the horizon have parted to grant me glimpses of the ways beyond; and sometimes at night the deep waters of the sea have grown clear and phosphorescent, to grant me glimpses of the ways beneath. And these glimpses have been as often of the ways that were and the ways that might be, as of the ways that are; for ocean is more ancient than the mountains, and freighted with the memories and the dreams of Time.

Out of the South it was that the White Ship used to come when the moon was full and high in the heavens. Out of the South it would glide very smoothly and silently over the sea. And whether the sea was rough or calm, and whether the wind was friendly or adverse, it would always glide smoothly and silently, its sails distent and its long strange tiers of oars moving rhythmically. One night I espied upon the deck a man, bearded and robed, and he seemed to beckon me to embark for fair unknown shores.

Many times afterward I saw him under the full moon, and ever did he beckon me.

Very brightly did the moon shine on the night I answered the call, and I walked out over the waters to the White Ship on a bridge of moonbeams. The man who had beckoned now spoke a welcome to me in a soft language I seemed to know well, and the hours were filled with soft songs of the oarsmen as we glided away into a mysterious South, golden with the glow of that full, mellow moon.

And when the day dawned, rosy and effulgent, I beheld the green shore of far lands, bright and beautiful, and to me unknown. Up from the sea rose lordly terraces of verdure, tree-studded, and shewing here and there the gleaming white roofs and colonnades of strange temples. As we drew nearer the green shore the bearded man told me of that land, the Land of Zar, where dwell all the dreams and thoughts of beauty that come to men once and then are forgotten. And when I looked upon the terraces again I saw that what he said was true, for among the sights before me were many things I had once seen through the mists beyond the horizon in the phosphorescent depths of ocean. There too were forms and fantasies more splendid than I had ever known; the visions of young poets who died in want before the world could learn of what they had seen and dreamed. But we did not set foot upon the sloping meadows of Zar, for it is told that he who

---

H.P. Lovecraft (1890-1937) authored *The Call of C'Thulhu* and several other horror classics, and was a regular contributor to *Weird Tales* and *Astounding Stories*. "The White Ship" originally appeared in *The United Amateur*, November 1919.

treads them may nevermore return to his native shore.

As the White Ship sailed silently away from the templed terraces of Zar, we beheld on the distant horizon ahead the spires of a mighty city; and the bearded man said to me, "This is Thalarion, the City of a Thousand Wonders, wherein reside all those mysteries that man has striven in vain to fathom." And I looked again, at closer range, and saw that the city was greater than any city I had known or dreamed of before. Into the sky the spires of its temples reached, so that no man might behold their peaks; and far back beyond the horizon stretched the grim, grey walls, over which one might spy only a few roofs, weird and ominous, yet adorned with rich friezes and alluring sculptures. I yearned mightily to enter this fascinating yet repellent city, and beseeched the bearded man to land me at the stone pier by the huge carven gate Akariel; but he gently denied my wish, saying, "Into Thalarion, the City of a Thousand Wonders, many have passed but none returned. Therein walk only dæmons and mad things that are no longer men, and the streets are white with the unburied bones of those who have looked upon the eidolon Lathi, that reigns over the city." So the White Ship sailed on past the walls of Thalarion, and followed for many days a southward-flying bird, whose glossy plumage matched the sky out of which it had appeared.

Then came we to a pleasant coast gay with blossoms of every hue, where as far inland as we could see basked lovely groves and radiant arbours beneath a meridian sun. From bowers beyond our view came bursts of song and snatches of lyric harmony, interspersed with faint laughter so delicious that I urged the rowers onward in my eagerness to reach the scene. And the bearded man spoke no word, but watched me as we approached the lily-lined shore. Suddenly a wind blowing from over the flowery meadows and leafy woods brought a scent at which I trembled. The wind grew stronger, and the air was filled with the lethal, charnel odour of plague-stricken towns and uncovered cemeteries. And as we sailed madly away from that damnable coast the bearded man spoke at last, saying, "This is Xura, the Land of Pleasures Unattained."

So once more the White Ship followed the bird of heaven, over warm blessed seas fanned by caressing, aromatic breezes. Day after day and night after night did we sail, and when the moon was full we would listen to soft songs of the oarsmen, sweet as on that distant night when we sailed away from my far native land. And it was by moonlight that we anchored at last in the harbour of Sona-Nyl, which is guarded by twin headlands of crystal that rise from the sea and meet in a resplendent arch. This is the Land of Fancy, and we walked to the verdant shore upon a golden bridge of moonbeams.

In the Land of Sona-Nyl there is neither time nor space, neither suffering nor death; and there I dwelt for many æons. Green are the groves and pastures, bright and fragrant the flowers, blue and musical the streams, clear and cool the fountains, and stately and gorgeous the temples, castles, and cities of Sona-Nyl. Of that land there is no bound, for beyond each vista of beauty rises another more beautiful. Over the countryside and amidst the splendour of cities can move at will the happy folk, of whom all are gifted with unmarred grace and unalloyed happiness. For the æons that I dwelt there I wandered blissfully through gardens where quaint pagodas peep from pleasing clumps of bushes, and where the white walks are bordered with delicate blossoms. I climbed gentle hills from whose summits I could see entrancing panoramas of loveliness, with steepled towns nestling in verdant valleys, and with the golden domes of gigantic cities glittering on the infinitely distant horizon. And I viewed by moonlight the sparkling sea, the crystal headlands, and the placid harbour wherein lay anchored the White Ship.

It was against the full moon one night in the immemorial year of Tharp that I saw outlined the beckoning form of the celestial bird, and felt the first stirrings of unrest. Then I spoke with the bearded man, and told him of my new yearning to depart for remote Cathuria, which no man hath seen, but which all believe to lie beyond the basalt pillars of the West. It is the Land of Hope, and in it shine the perfect ideals of all that we know elsewhere; or at least so men relate. But the bearded man said to me, "Beware of those perilous seas wherein men say Cathuria lies. In Sona-Nyl there is no pain nor death, but who can tell what lies beyond the basalt pillars of the West?" Natheless at the next full moon I boarded the White Ship, and with the reluctant bearded man left the happy harbour for untravelled seas.

And the bird of heaven flew before, and led us toward the basalt pillars of the West, but this time the oarsmen sang no soft songs under the full moon. In my mind I would often picture the unknown Land of Cathuria with its splendid groves and palaces, and would wonder what new delights there awaited me. "Cathuria," I would say to myself, "is the abode of gods and the land of unnumbered cities of gold. Its forests are of aloe and sandalwood, even as the fragrant groves of Camorin, and among the trees flutter gay birds sweet with song. On the green and flowery mountains of Cathuria stand temples of pink marble, rich with carven and painted glories, and having in their courtyards cool fountains of silver, where purl with ravishing music the scented waters that come from the grotto-born river Narg. And the cities of Cathuria are cinctured with golden walls, and their pavements are also of gold. In the gardens of these cities are strange orchids, and perfumed lakes whose beds are of coral and amber. At night the streets and the gardens are lit with gay lanthorns fashioned from three-coloured shell of the tortoise, and here resound the soft notes of the singer and the lutanist. And the houses of the cities of Cathuria are all palaces, each built over a fragrant canal bearing the waters of the sacred Narg. Of marble and porphyry are the houses, and roofed with glittering gold that reflects the rays of the sun and enhances the splendour of the cities as blissful gods view them from the distant peaks. Fairest of all is the palace of the great monarch Dorieb, whom some say to be a demigod and others a god. High is the palace of Dorieb, and many are the turrets of marble upon its walls. In its wide halls may multitudes assemble, and here hang the trophies of the ages. And the roof is of pure gold, set upon tall pillars of ruby and azure, and having such carven figures of gods and heroes that he who looks up to those heights seem to gaze upon the living Olympus. And the floor of the palace is of glass, under which flow the cunningly lighted waters of the Narg, gay with gaudy fish not known beyond the bounds of lovely Cathuria."

Thus would I speak to myself of Cathuria, but ever would the bearded man warn me to turn back to the happy shores of Sona-Nyl; for Sona-Nyl is known of men, while none hath ever beheld Cathuria.

And on the thirty-first day that we followed the bird, we beheld the basalt pillars of the West. Shrouded in mist they were, so that no man might peer beyond them or see their summits—which indeed some say reach even to the heavens. And the bearded man again implored me to turn back, but I heeded him not; for from the mists beyond the basalt pillars I fancied there came the notes of singer and lutanist; sweeter than the sweetest songs of Sona-Nyl, and sounding mine own praises; the praises of me, who had voyaged far under the full moon and dwelt in the Land of Fancy.

So to the sound of melody the White Ship sailed into the mist betwixt the basalt pillars of the West. And when the music ceased and the mist lifted, we beheld not the Land of Cathuria, but a swift-rushing resistless sea, over which our helpless barque was borne toward some unknown goal. Soon to our ears came the distant thunder of falling waters, and to our eyes appeared on the far horizon ahead the titanic spray of a monstrous cataract, wherein the oceans of the world drop down to abysmal nothingness. Then did the bearded man say to me with tears on his cheek, "We have rejected the beautiful Land of Sona-Nyl, which we may never behold again. The gods are greater than men, and they have conquered." And I closed my eyes before the crash that I knew would come, shutting out the sight of the celestial bird which flapped its mocking blue wings over the brink of the torrent.

Out of that crash came darkness, and I heard the shrieking of men and of things which were not men. From the East tempestuous winds arose, and chilled me as I crouched on the slab of damp stone which had risen beneath my feet. Then as I heard another crash I opened my eyes and beheld myself upon the platform of that lighthouse from whence I had sailed so many æons ago. In the darkness below there loomed the vast blurred outlines of a vessel breaking up on the cruel rocks, and as I glanced out over the waste I saw that the light had failed for the first time since my grandfather had assumed its care.

And in the later watches of the night, when I went within the tower, I saw on the wall a calendar which still remained as when I had left it at the hour I sailed away. With the dawn I descended the tower and looked for wreckage upon the rocks, but what I found was only this: a strange dead bird whose hue was as of the azure sky, and a single shattered spar, of a whiteness greater than that of the wave-tips or of the mountain snow.

And thereafter the ocean told me its secrets no more; and though many times since has the moon shone full and high in the heavens, the White Ship from the South came never again. ■

JUNE
15

The Tunnel Under the World

56

The Tunnel Under The World

**Pinching yourself is no way to see if you are dreaming.
Surgical instruments? Well, yes-but a mechanic's kit is best of all!**

By FREDERIK POHL

Illustrated by EMSH

ON THE morning of June 15th, Guy Burckhardt woke up screaming out of a dream.

It was more real than any dream he had ever had in his life. He could still hear and feel the sharp, ripping-metal explosion, the violent heave that had tossed him furiously out of bed, the searing wave of heat.

He sat up convulsively and stared, not believing what he saw, at the quiet room and the bright sunlight coming in the window.

He croaked, "Mary?"

His wife was not in the bed next to him. The covers were tumbled and awry, as though she had just left it, and the memory of the dream was so strong that instinctively he found himself searching the floor to see if the dream explosion had thrown her down.

But she wasn't there. Of course she wasn't, he told himself, looking at the familiar vanity and slipper chair, the uncracked window, the unbuckled wall. It had only been a dream.

"Guy?" His wife was calling him querulously from the foot of the stairs. "Guy, dear, are you all right?"

He called weakly, "Sure."

There was a pause. Then Mary said doubtfully, "Breakfast is ready. Are you sure you're all right? I thought I heard you yelling—"

Burckhardt said more confidently, "I had a bad dream, honey. Be right down."

In the shower, punching the lukewarm-and-cologne he favored, he told himself that it had been a beaut of a dream. Still, bad dreams weren't unusual, especially bad dreams about explosions. In the past thirty years of H-bomb jitters, who had not dreamed of explosions?

Even Mary had dreamed of them, it turned out, for he started to tell her about the dream, but she cut him off. "You *did*?" Her voice was astonished. "Why, dear, I dreamed the same thing! Well, almost the same thing. I didn't actually *hear* anything. I dreamed that something woke me up, and then there was a sort of quick bang, and then something hit me on the head. And that was all. Was yours like that?"

Burckhardt coughed. "Well, no," he said. Mary was not one of these strong-as-a-man, brave-as-a-tiger women. It was not necessary, he thought, to tell her all the little details of the dream that made it seem

57

so real. No need to mention the splintered ribs, and the salt bubble in his throat, and the agonized knowledge that this was death. He said, "Maybe there really was some kind of explosion downtown. Maybe we heard it and it started us dreaming."

Mary reached over and patted his hand absently. "Maybe," she agreed. "It's almost half-past eight, dear. Shouldn't you hurry? You don't want to be late to the office."

He gulped his food, kissed her and rushed out—not so much to be on time as to see if his guess had been right.

But downtown Tylerton looked as it always had. Coming in on the bus, Burckhardt watched critically out the window, seeking evidence of an explosion. There wasn't any. If anything, Tylerton looked better than it ever had before: It was a beautiful crisp day, the sky was cloudless, the buildings were clean and inviting. They had, he observed, steam-blasted the Power & Light Building, the town's only skyscraper—that was the penalty of having Contro Chemical's main plant on the outskirts of town; the fumes from the cascade stills left their mark on stone buildings.

None of the usual crowd were on the bus, so there wasn't anyone Burckhardt could ask about the explosion. And by the time he got out at the corner of Fifth and Lehigh and the bus rolled away with a muted diesel moan, he had pretty well convinced himself that it was all imagination.

He stopped at the cigar stand in the lobby of his office building, but Ralph wasn't behind the counter. The man who sold him his pack of cigarettes was a stranger.

"Where's Mr. Stebbins?" Burckhardt asked.

The man said politely, "Sick, sir. He'll be in tomorrow. A pack of Marlins today?"

"Chesterfields," Burckhardt corrected.

"Certainly, sir," the man said. But what he took from the rack and slid across the counter was an unfamiliar green-and-yellow pack.

"Do try these, sir," he suggested. "They contain an anti-cough factor. Ever notice how ordinary cigarettes make you choke every once in a while?"

Burckhardt said suspiciously, "I never heard of this brand."

"Of course not. They're something new." Burckhardt hesitated, and the man said persuasively, "Look, try them out at my risk. If you don't like them, bring back the empty pack and I'll refund your money. Fair enough?"

Burckhardt shrugged. "How can I lose? But give me a pack of Chesterfields, too, will you?"

***

Frederik Pohl (1919 -2013) wrote science fiction for 75-plus years. He edited *Galaxy* magazine, won three Hugo Awards and three Nebula Awards, among others. He was inducted into the Science Fiction and Fantasy Hall of Fame (1998) and won a Hugo Award for Best Fan Writer for "The Way the Future Blogs." "Tunnel Under the World" originally appeared in *Galaxy,*

He opened the pack and lit one while he waited for the elevator. They weren't bad, he decided, though he was suspicious of cigarettes that had the tobacco chemically treated in any way. But he didn't think much of Ralph's stand-in; it would raise hell with the trade at the cigar stand if the man tried to give every customer the same high-pressure sales talk.

The elevator door opened with a low-pitched sound of music. Burckhardt and two or three others got in and he nodded to them as the door closed. The thread of music switched off and the speaker in the ceiling of the cab began its usual commercials.

No, not the *usual* commercials, Burckhardt realized. He had been exposed to the captive-audience commercials so long that they hardly registered on the outer ear any more, but what was coming from the recorded program in the basement of the building caught his attention. It wasn't merely that the brands were mostly unfamiliar; it was a difference in pattern.

There were jingles with an insistent, bouncy rhythm, about soft drinks he had never tasted. There was a rapid patter dialogue between what sounded like two ten-year-old boys about a candy bar, followed by an authoritative bass rumble: "Go right out and get a DELICIOUS Choco-Bite and eat your TANGY Choco-Bite *all up*. That's *Choco-Bite*!" There was a sobbing female whine: "I *wish* I had a Feckle Freezer! I'd do *anything* for a Feckle Freezer!" Burckhardt reached his floor and left the elevator in the middle of the last one. It left him a little uneasy. The commercials were not for familiar brands; there

was no feeling of use and custom to them.

But the office was happily normal—except that Mr. Barth wasn't in. Miss Mitkin, yawning at the reception desk, didn't know exactly why. "His home phoned, that's all. He'll be in tomorrow."

"Maybe he went to the plant. It's right near his house."

She looked indifferent. "Yeah."

A thought struck Burckhardt. "But today is June 15th! It's quarterly tax return day—he has to sign the return!"

Miss Mitkin shrugged to indicate that that was Burckhardt's problem, not hers. She returned to her nails.

Thoroughly exasperated, Burckhardt went to his desk. It wasn't that he couldn't sign the tax returns as well as Barth, he thought resentfully. It simply wasn't his job, that was all; it was a responsibility that Barth, as office manager for Contro Chemicals' downtown office, should have taken.

He thought briefly of calling Barth at his home or trying to reach him at the factory, but he gave up the idea quickly enough. He didn't really care much for the people at the factory and the less contact he had with them, the better. He had been to the factory once, with Barth; it had been a confusing and, in a way, a frightening experience. Barring a handful of executives and engineers, there wasn't a soul in the factory—that is, Burckhardt corrected himself, remembering what Barth had told him, not a *living* soul—just the machines.

According to Barth, each machine was controlled by a sort of computer which reproduced, in its electronic snarl, the actual memory and mind of a human being. It was an unpleasant thought. Barth, laughing, had assured him that there was no Frankenstein business of robbing graveyards and implanting brains in machines. It was only a matter, he said, of transferring a man's habit patterns from brain cells to vacuum-tube cells. It didn't hurt the man and it didn't make the machine into a monster.

But they made Burckhardt uncomfortable all the same.

He put Barth and the factory and all his other little irritations out of his mind and tackled the tax returns. It took him until noon to verify the figures—which Barth could have done out of his memory and his private ledger in ten minutes, Burckhardt resentfully reminded himself.

He sealed them in an envelope and walked out to Miss Mitkin. "Since Mr. Barth isn't here, we'd better go to lunch in shifts," he said. "You can go first."

"Thanks." Miss Mitkin languidly took her bag out of the desk drawer and began to apply makeup.

Burckhardt offered her the envelope. "Drop this in the mail for me, will you? Uh—wait a minute. I wonder if I ought to phone Mr. Barth to make sure. Did his wife say whether he was able to take phone calls?"

"Didn't say." Miss Mitkin blotted her lips carefully with a Kleenex. "Wasn't his wife, anyway. It was his daughter who called and left the message."

"The kid?" Burckhardt frowned. "I thought she was away at school."

"She called, that's all I know."

Burckhardt went back to his own office and stared distastefully at the unopened mail on his desk. He didn't like nightmares; they spoiled his whole day. He should have stayed in bed, like Barth.

A funny thing happened on his way home. There was a disturbance at the corner where he usually caught his bus—someone was screaming something about a new kind of deep-freeze—so he walked an extra block. He saw the bus coming and started to trot. But behind him, someone was calling his name. He looked over his shoulder; a small harried-looking man was hurrying toward him.

Burckhardt hesitated, and then recognized him. It was a casual acquaintance named Swanson. Burckhardt sourly observed that he had already missed the bus.

He said, "Hello."

Swanson's face was desperately eager. "Burckhardt?" he asked inquiringly, with an odd intensity. And then he just stood there silently, watching Burckhardt's face, with a burning eagerness that dwindled to a faint hope and died to a regret. He was searching for something, waiting for something, Burckhardt thought. But whatever it was he wanted, Burckhardt didn't know how to supply it.

Burckhardt coughed and said again, "Hello, Swanson."

Swanson didn't even acknowledge the greeting. He merely sighed a very deep sigh.

"Nothing doing," he mumbled, apparently to himself. He nodded abstractedly to Burckhardt and turned away.

Burckhardt watched the slumped

shoulders disappear in the crowd. It was an *odd* sort of day, he thought, and one he didn't much like. Things weren't going right.

Riding home on the next bus, he brooded about it. It wasn't anything terrible or disastrous; it was something out of his experience entirely. You live your life, like any man, and you form a network of impressions and reactions. You *expect* things. When you open your medicine chest, your razor is expected to be on the second shelf; when you lock your front door, you expect to have to give it a slight extra tug to make it latch.

It isn't the things that are right and perfect in your life that make it familiar. It is the things that are just a little bit wrong— the sticking latch, the light switch at the head of the stairs that needs an extra push because the spring is old and weak, the rug that unfailingly skids underfoot.

It wasn't just that things were wrong with the pattern of Burckhardt's life; it was that the *wrong* things were wrong. For instance, Barth hadn't come into the office, yet Barth *always* came in.

Burckhardt brooded about it through dinner. He brooded about it, despite his wife's attempt to interest him in a game of bridge with the neighbors, all through the evening. The neighbors were people he liked—Anne and Farley Dennerman. He had known them all their lives. But they were odd and brooding, too, this night and he barely listened to Dennerman's complaints about not being able to get good phone service or his wife's comments on the disgusting variety of television commercials they had these days.

Burckhardt was well on the way to setting an all-time record for continuous abstraction when, around midnight, with a suddenness that surprised him—he was strangely *aware* of it happening—he turned over in his bed and, quickly and completely, fell asleep.

II

On the morning of June 15th, Burckhardt woke up screaming.

It was more real than any dream he had ever had in his life. He could still hear the explosion, feel the blast that crushed him against a wall. It did not seem right that he should be sitting bolt upright in bed in an undisturbed room.

His wife came pattering up the stairs. "Darling!" she cried. "What's the matter?"

He mumbled, "Nothing. Bad dream."

She relaxed, hand on heart. In an angry tone, she started to say: "You gave me such a shock—"

But a noise from outside interrupted her. There was a wail of sirens and a clang of bells; it was loud and shocking.

The Burckhardts stared at each other for a heartbeat, then hurried fearfully to the window.

There were no rumbling fire engines in the street, only a small panel truck, cruising slowly along. Flaring loudspeaker horns crowned its top. From them issued the screaming sound of sirens, growing in intensity, mixed with the rumble of heavy-duty engines and the sound of bells. It was a perfect record of fire engines arriving at a four-alarm blaze.

Burckhardt said in amazement, "Mary,

that's against the law! Do you know what they're doing? They're playing records of a fire. What are they up to?"

"Maybe it's a practical joke," his wife offered.

"Joke? Waking up the whole neighborhood at six o'clock in the morning?" He shook his head. "The police will be here in ten minutes," he predicted. "Wait and see."

But the police weren't—not in ten minutes, or at all. Whoever the pranksters in the car were, they apparently had a police permit for their games.

The car took a position in the middle of the block and stood silent for a few minutes. Then there was a crackle from the speaker, and a giant voice chanted:

"Feckle Freezers! Feckle Freezers! Gotta have a Feckle Freezer! Feckle, Feckle, Feckle, Feckle, Feckle, Feckle—"

It went on and on. Every house on the block had faces staring out of windows by then. The voice was not merely loud; it was nearly deafening.

Burckhardt shouted to his wife, over the uproar, "What the hell is a Feckle Freezer?"

"Some kind of a freezer, I guess, dear," she shrieked back unhelpfully.

Abruptly the noise stopped and the truck stood silent. It was still misty morning; the Sun's rays came horizontally across the rooftops. It was impossible to believe that, a moment ago, the silent block had been bellowing the name of a freezer.

"A crazy advertising trick," Burckhardt said bitterly. He yawned and turned away from the window. "Might as well get dressed. I guess that's the end of—"

The bellow caught him from behind; it was almost like a hard slap on the ears. A harsh, sneering voice, louder than the archangel's trumpet, howled:

"Have you got a freezer? *It stinks!* If it isn't a Feckle Freezer, *it stinks*! If it's a last year's Feckle Freezer, *it stinks*! Only this year's Feckle Freezer is any good at all! You know who owns an Ajax Freezer? Fairies own Ajax Freezers! You know who owns a Triplecold Freezer? Commies own Triplecold Freezers! Every freezer but a brand-new Feckle Freezer *stinks*!"

The voice screamed inarticulately with rage. "I'm warning you! Get out and buy a Feckle Freezer right away! Hurry up! Hurry for Feckle! Hurry for Feckle! Hurry, hurry, hurry, Feckle, Feckle, Feckle, Feckle, Feckle, Feckle...."

It stopped eventually. Burckhardt licked his lips. He started to say to his wife, "Maybe we ought to call the police about—" when the speakers erupted again. It caught him off guard; it was intended to catch him off guard. It screamed:

"Feckle, Feckle, Feckle, Feckle, Feckle, Feckle, Feckle, Feckle. Cheap freezers ruin your food. You'll get sick and throw up. You'll get sick and die. Buy a Feckle, Feckle, Feckle, Feckle! Ever take a piece of meat out of the freezer you've got and see how rotten and moldy it is? Buy a Feckle, Feckle, Feckle, Feckle, Feckle. Do you want to eat rotten, stinking food? Or do you want to wise up and buy a Feckle, Feckle, Feckle—"

That did it. With fingers that kept stabbing the wrong holes, Burckhardt finally managed to dial the local police station. He got a busy signal—it was apparent that he was not the only one with the same idea—and while he was shakingly dialing again, the noise outside stopped.

He looked out the window. The truck was gone.

Burckhardt loosened his tie and ordered another Frosty-Flip from the waiter. If only they wouldn't keep the Crystal Cafe so *hot*! The new paint job—searing reds and blinding yellows—was bad enough, but someone seemed to have the delusion that this was January instead of June; the place was a good ten degrees warmer than outside.

He swallowed the Frosty-Flip in two gulps. It had a kind of peculiar flavor, he thought, but not bad. It certainly cooled you off, just as the waiter had promised. He reminded himself to pick up a carton of them on the way home; Mary might like them. She was always interested in something new.

He stood up awkwardly as the girl came across the restaurant toward him. She was the most beautiful thing he had ever seen in Tylerton. Chin-height, honey-blonde hair and a figure that—well, it was all hers. There was no doubt in the world that the dress that clung to her was the only thing she wore. He felt as if he were blushing as she greeted him.

"Mr. Burckhardt." The voice was like distant tomtoms. "It's wonderful of you to let me see you, after this morning."

He cleared his throat. "Not at all. Won't you sit down, Miss—"

"April Horn," she murmured, sitting down—beside him, not where he had pointed on the other side of the table. "Call me April, won't you?"

She was wearing some kind of perfume, Burckhardt noted with what little of his mind was functioning at all. It didn't seem fair that she should be using perfume as well as everything else. He came to with a start and realized that the waiter was leaving with an order for *filets mignon* for two.

"Hey!" he objected.

"Please, Mr. Burckhardt." Her shoulder was against his, her face was turned to him, her breath was warm, her expression was tender and solicitous. "This is all on the Feckle Corporation. Please let them—it's the *least* they can do."

He felt her hand burrowing into his pocket.

"I put the price of the meal into your pocket," she whispered conspiratorially. "Please do that for me, won't you? I mean I'd appreciate it if you'd pay the waiter—I'm old-fashioned about things like that."

She smiled meltingly, then became mock-businesslike. "But you must take the money," she insisted. "Why, you're letting Feckle off lightly if you do! You could sue them for every nickel they've got, disturbing your sleep like that."

With a dizzy feeling, as though he had just seen someone make a rabbit disappear into a top hat, he said, "Why, it really wasn't so bad, uh, April. A little noisy, maybe, but—"

"Oh, Mr. Burckhardt!" The blue eyes were wide and admiring. "I knew you'd understand. It's just that—well, it's such a *wonderful* freezer that some of the outside men get carried away, so to speak. As soon as the main office found out about what happened, they sent representatives around to every house on the block to apologize. Your wife told us where we could phone you—and I'm so very pleased that you were willing to let me have lunch with you, so that I could apologize, too. Because truly, Mr. Burckhardt, it is a *fine* freezer.

"I shouldn't tell you this, but—" the blue eyes were shyly lowered—"I'd do almost anything for Feckle Freezers. It's more than a job to me." She looked up. She was enchanting. "I bet you think I'm silly, don't you?"

Burckhardt coughed. "Well, I—"

"Oh, you don't want to be unkind!" She shook her head. "No, don't pretend. You think it's silly. But really, Mr. Burckhardt, you wouldn't think so if you knew more about the Feckle. Let me show you this little booklet—"

Burckhardt got back from lunch a full hour late. It wasn't only the girl who delayed him. There had been a curious interview with a little man named Swanson, whom he barely knew, who had stopped him with desperate urgency on the street—and then left him cold.

But it didn't matter much. Mr. Barth, for the first time since Burckhardt had worked there, was out for the day—leaving Burckhardt stuck with the quarterly tax returns.

What did matter, though, was that somehow he had signed a purchase order for a twelve-cubic-foot Feckle Freezer, upright model, self-defrosting, list price $625, with a ten per cent "courtesy" discount—"Because of that *horrid* affair this morning, Mr. Burckhardt," she had said.

And he wasn't sure how he could explain it to his wife.

He needn't have worried. As he walked in the front door, his wife said almost immediately, "I wonder if we can't afford a new freezer, dear. There was a man here to apologize about that noise and—well, we got to talking and—"

She had signed a purchase order, too.

It had been the damnedest day, Burckhardt thought later, on his way up to bed. But the day wasn't done with him yet. At the head of the stairs, the weakened spring in the electric light switch refused to click at all. He snapped it back and forth angrily and, of course, succeeded in jarring the tumbler out of its pins. The wires shorted and every light in the house went out.

"Damn!" said Guy Burckhardt.

"Fuse?" His wife shrugged sleepily. "Let it go till the morning, dear."

Burckhardt shook his head. "You go back to bed. I'll be right along."

It wasn't so much that he cared about fixing the fuse, but he was too restless for sleep. He disconnected the bad switch with a screwdriver, stumbled down into the black kitchen, found the flashlight and climbed gingerly down the cellar stairs. He located a spare fuse, pushed an empty trunk over to the fuse box to stand on and twisted out the old fuse.

When the new one was in, he heard the starting click and steady drone of the refrigerator in the kitchen overhead.

He headed back to the steps, and stopped.

Where the old trunk had been, the cellar

floor gleamed oddly bright. He inspected it in the flashlight beam. It was metal!

"Son of a gun," said Guy Burckhardt. He shook his head unbelievingly. He peered closer, rubbed the edges of the metallic patch with his thumb and acquired an annoying cut—the edges were *sharp*.

The stained cement floor of the cellar was a thin shell. He found a hammer and cracked it off in a dozen spots—everywhere was metal.

The whole cellar was a copper box. Even the cement-brick walls were false fronts over a metal sheath!

Baffled, he attacked one of the foundation beams. That, at least, was real wood. The glass in the cellar windows was real glass.

He sucked his bleeding thumb and tried the base of the cellar stairs. Real wood. He chipped at the bricks under the oil burner. Real bricks. The retaining walls, the floor—they were faked.

It was as though someone had shored up the house with a frame of metal and then laboriously concealed the evidence.

The biggest surprise was the upside-down boat hull that blocked the rear half of the cellar, relic of a brief home workshop period that Burckhardt had gone through a couple of years before. From above, it looked perfectly normal. Inside, though, where there should have been thwarts and seats and lockers, there was a mere tangle of braces, rough and unfinished.

"But I *built* that!" Burckhardt exclaimed, forgetting his thumb. He leaned against the hull dizzily, trying to think this thing through. For reasons beyond his comprehension, someone had taken his boat and his cellar away, maybe his whole house, and replaced them with a clever mock-up of the real thing.

"That's crazy," he said to the empty cellar. He stared around in the light of the flash. He whispered, "What in the name of Heaven would anybody do that for?"

Reason refused an answer; there wasn't any reasonable answer. For long minutes, Burckhardt contemplated the uncertain picture of his own sanity.

He peered under the boat again, hoping to reassure himself that it was a mistake, just his imagination. But the sloppy, unfinished bracing was unchanged. He crawled under for a better look, feeling the rough wood incredulously. Utterly impossible!

He switched off the flashlight and started to wriggle out. But he didn't make it. In the moment between the command to his legs to move and the crawling out, he felt a sudden draining weariness flooding through him.

Consciousness went—not easily, but as though it were being taken away, and Guy Burckhardt was asleep.

III

On the morning of June 16th, Guy Burckhardt woke up in a cramped position huddled under the hull of the boat in his basement—and raced upstairs to find it was June 15th.

The first thing he had done was to make a frantic, hasty inspection of the boat hull, the faked cellar floor, the imitation stone. They were all as he had remembered them—all completely unbelievable.

The kitchen was its placid, unexciting

self. The electric clock was purring soberly around the dial. Almost six o'clock, it said. His wife would be waking at any moment.

Burckhardt flung open the front door and stared out into the quiet street. The morning paper was tossed carelessly against the steps—and as he retrieved it, he noticed that this was the 15th day of June.

But that was impossible. *Yesterday* was the 15th of June. It was not a date one would forget—it was quarterly tax-return day.

He went back into the hall and picked up the telephone; he dialed for Weather Information, and got a well-modulated chant: "—and cooler, some showers. Barometric pressure thirty point zero four, rising ... United States Weather Bureau forecast for June 15th. Warm and sunny, with high around—"

He hung the phone up. June 15th.

"Holy heaven!" Burckhardt said prayerfully. Things were very odd indeed. He heard the ring of his wife's alarm and bounded up the stairs.

Mary Burckhardt was sitting upright in bed with the terrified, uncomprehending stare of someone just waking out of a nightmare.

"Oh!" she gasped, as her husband came in the room. "Darling, I just had the most *terrible* dream! It was like an explosion and—"

"Again?" Burckhardt asked, not very sympathetically. "Mary, something's funny! I *knew* there was something wrong all day yesterday and—"

He went on to tell her about the copper box that was the cellar, and the odd mock-up someone had made of his boat. Mary looked astonished, then alarmed, then placatory and uneasy.

She said, "Dear, are you *sure*? Because I was cleaning that old trunk out just last week and I didn't notice anything."

"Positive!" said Guy Burckhardt. "I dragged it over to the wall to step on it to put a new fuse in after we blew the lights out and—"

"After we what?" Mary was looking more than merely alarmed.

"After we blew the lights out. You know, when the switch at the head of the stairs stuck. I went down to the cellar and—"

Mary sat up in bed. "Guy, the switch didn't stick. I turned out the lights myself last night."

Burckhardt glared at his wife. "Now I *know* you didn't! Come here and take a look!"

He stalked out to the landing and dramatically pointed to the bad switch, the one that he had unscrewed and left hanging the night before....

Only it wasn't. It was as it had always been. Unbelieving, Burckhardt pressed it and the lights sprang up in both halls.

Mary, looking pale and worried, left him to go down to the kitchen and start breakfast. Burckhardt stood staring at the switch for a long time. His mental processes were gone beyond the point of disbelief and shock; they simply were not functioning.

He shaved and dressed and ate his breakfast in a state of numb introspection. Mary didn't disturb him; she was (Continued on page 101)

■ ■ ■

"He was a pain in the ass," the F.B.I. agent who identified himself as Muldoon said. "To be more specific, he was a pain in *my* ass for years."

The "he" Muldoon spoke of was Rodney Field, conspiracy theorist extraordinaire. Up until his recent death, Field had been the most prolific spreader of conspiracies in North America, having explained the assassination of J.F.K. alone in more than fifty different ways.

He started in the 1950's, self-publishing his bizarre little booklets, theorizing on everything from Macarthyism to Lucille Ball, occasionally connecting the two. He should have drifted into obscurity years ago, but some idiot invented the internet, another idiot taught Field how to use it, and thousands of idiots read his ranting on a regular basis. Many of Field's readers also read the supermarket tabloid that kept food on my table, which led me to sitting across a table from Muldoon in his office.

CONSPIRACYTHEORY

BY CARSON DEMANNS

"Every Thursday," Muldoon continued," that crazy little bastard would park his scrawny ass in the same chair you're sitting in now and torture me with the craziest shit he could come up with. Don't ask me how many years he did it because I'm trying to block it out."

"What did he talk about?" I asked.

"It doesn't matter," Muldoon said dismissively.

"Then why did the F.B.I. arrest him a week before he died? Why seize all of his personal papers and his hard drives?"

"None of your business," Muldoon said. He stretched as he yawned. "You can leave now."

"Maybe I should talk to another agent," I said. "Does a Rodney work here?"

"The only Rodney who ever came around here was Field."

"Then why is there a personalized coffee mug labelled Rodney on the shelf behind you?"

Muldoon was suddenly no longer sleepy. He sprung to attention in his swivel chair and quickly spun it around. He grabbed the mug, turned around again to face me, and shoved the mug in a drawer in the table between the two of us.

"Just junk," Muldoon muttered.

"Then why are you saving it instead of throwing it out?" I asked.

Muldoon raised his overweight frame out of his chair and firmly put a hand on my shoulder. He turned my chair around so I faced the door. I took the hint and left.

My next stop was the old apartment building Field had called home for the last years of his life. Places like that are always owned by numbered companies which are in turn owned by business people who gladly collect the rent without ever seeing the dumps they own and managed by poor slobs who need the cheap apartments the owners provide and are glad to supplement their incomes with one of the five dollar bills I always keep in my pocket.

"Sure I remember Field." The balding manager suddenly remembered after he put my money in his pants. "He always said he was onto something, and I guess he really was."

"Why do you say that?"

"Because he always said they'd come for him and they finally did," the manager said. "A week later he was dead, and those feds cleaned his place out so thoroughly I could have rented it the next day."

"What did the feds take?" I asked.

"Everything. The old guy crammed the place with all kinds of crap. Books, journals, photos, newspapers, you name it."

"Did anyone ever come see him when he was alive?"

"Not really. Some fat guy used to drop by once in a while to see how he was. Mulligan or Milligan or something like that."

"Muldoon?" I asked.

"Could be," the manager nodded. "Since Field died all kinds of people have come by though. I never even knew Field

---

Carson Demanns is a long-time gag writer and the author of four published books, and has appeared before in *Pulp Adventures*.

had a kid until he stopped by a couple of days ago."

"Field had a son?" I asked in amazement. Nothing in my research had shown that.

"Apparently," the manager said. "But the kid had a different last name. He left me a business card, but I don't know where I put it."

Leo Miller's business card magically appeared in the manager's hand when another five-dollar bill appeared in mine. Miller was anxious to talk to me when I called him and we arranged to meet in a nearby coffee shop. I planned on asking him some questions about Field, but instead he began asking me questions as soon as he had jumped out of his car and ran up to where I was sitting.

"I've been robbed!" Miller gasped. "Can you help me?"

"What were you robbed of?" I asked.

"Everything," Miller said. "Everything my father was going to leave me."

"Who was your father?" I asked.

"A great man," he said. "Ronald Field."

"How do I know you are his son?" I asked. Miller opened his briefcase and provided me with documents showing that he had been born Ronald Field Junior before legally changing his name years ago.

"You must not have thought he was that great when you changed your name."

Miller blushed slightly. It would have been funny on a child and attractive on a woman but was simply silly-looking on a middle-aged man.

"I didn't understand my father when he was alive," Miller admitted. "Nobody

did. Look, I'll admit most people thought my father was a crackpot, and for most of my life I thought the same thing. No matter how many times I got different unlisted telephone numbers, he'd find me and call at all hours and tell me his latest theory. I thought it was all crap, but now he's dead and his life's work is gone."

"Unlisted phone numbers are hard to find," I said. "How did he find your's?"

Miller laughed.

"He claimed the F.B.I. found me for him," Miller replied. "The F.B.I. came to my house after my father died to see if he had stored anything there. I wish he had given me something before he died. There's been a lot of demand for anything related to his work."

"What do you mean?"

"Do you think you're the only one writing about him? Google him," Miller suggested. "Rodney Field is now a conspiracy theory legend. There are hundreds of websites devoted to him now, all wondering what he stumbled onto before the government got him."

"Do you remember anything about the F.B.I. agent who came to see you?"

"Not really," Miller said. "Some big fat guy. He seemed to know my dad pretty well. He probably has a file on my family a foot thick."

"Describe your dad to me. You must have hated him a lot at one point in your life to have changed your name the way you did."

Miller nodded his head in a combination of regret and acknowledgement.

"In small doses, everyone loved my dad. He was funny, smart and had a wild imagination. But you can't have a dad in small doses."

"So he'd be a great guy to have coffee with once a week?"

"I suppose," Miller agreed.

"Do you know what your dad died of?"

"I don't know exactly. He went to a clinic every week for something. I can give you its name if you want."

I wanted the name and Miller gave it to me in exchange for a promise to give him anything of his father's that I found. I called the clinic, and they couldn't tell me much other than Field had lots of health problems that eventually caught up to him.

They also said Field was usually driven there by his friend, Mr. Muldoon.

I googled Field as his son had suggested. He now had a cult following bigger than the dead presidents whose deaths he had tried to explain during his life. The websites told me more about Muldoon than they did about Field.

Muldoon was an unlovable jerk, but he had obviously liked Field enough to buy the old guy his own mug for their weekly chats, and chauffeured Field around. The only interesting fact on the websites was Field's birthday, the last one of which coincided with the date Muldoon arrested his only friend and seized all of his property.

I realized from the hundreds of websites celebrating an old man whose death was inevitable that it was on that day Muldoon had given his friend the greatest birthday gift you can give a dying man: immortality. ∎

CAPTAIN WARWICK'S HAND

by Adam Beau McFarlane

A tropical tempest emptied the pirate town Blackport. Streets cleared and sailors waited in docked ships. Vast black clouds hid the sun. Rain and cold air pushed down on the harbor. The squall covered the island.

Cobbled together from broken masts, the ramshackle tavern's frame shook and shuddered. Walls of ripped canvas sails did little to stop a frigid draft from seeping in. The air was smoky from an attempt to start a fire, stamped out before its rising heat and drying air put flame to the ceiling. A charred stench infused the air.

I longed to be home with Da and my sister, beside the hearth and sharing a warm apple brandy. Instead, I bartended for ruffians and ne'er-do-wells. A pot of water boiled. With various spirits, I poured hot water and flavorings — cinnamon, sugarcane, cloves, lemon, and gratings of ginger root.

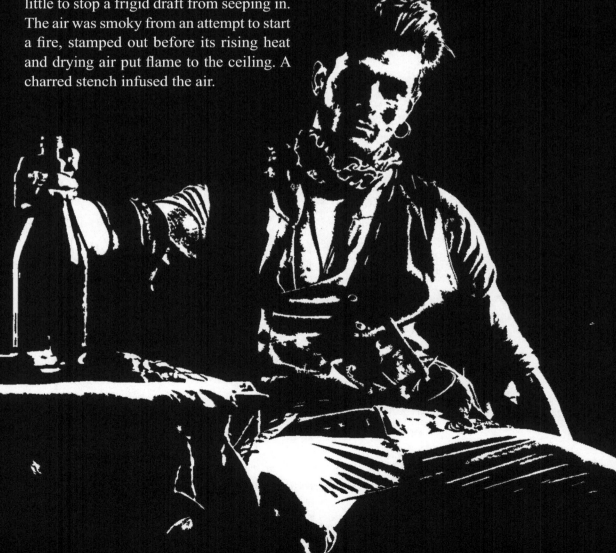

Stories from Blackport Island Tavern

Men clutched cups with both hands to warm their fingers. Waiting for their clothes and backsides to dry, they muttered. It was a low time that soured moods. Weather put aches in the joints of old pirates who groaned about them, while others shared their own suffering.

"I have no money left," Quinton whined. The purple kerchief knotted around his head was soaked, and his tunic was worn to rags. Hard years had spoiled his face like a piece of fruit — yellowed and wrinkled, and some of his teeth were missing or blackened by decay. He was fifty years of age, if he was a day. "How will I eat?"

"You shouldn't have spent it all on drink," Palgrave said, gazing at the dregs of spices and rind settling at the bottom of his glass. He was pale from face powder, and his wig was maintained neatly. Palgrave was in his thirties, though the powder covered any aging to his complexion. How he kept his crimson beefeater's robe spotless, I'll never know.

"If I'd stayed on the farm," Quinton said. "I'd have never worried about money for food, nor ever gone hungry."

"If you'd kept on the farm, all of us would have suffered less," Palgrave replied.

"Enough squabble!" Captain Warwick grumbled. He glared with his one eye. The striped, honey-colored gem set in the other socket gleamed. His prominent nose cut the air like a hawk's beak. Salt and pepper hair ran from his tricorn hat down his chin to a shaggy beard.

Quinton silenced himself and looked away, but Warwick went on. "So, you were a farmer, then? What of storms? Or droughts or vermin? Did you not pay for your life by servitude to the earth? And you, Palgrave, ought to be ashamed. What do you expect from a farmer who lived by barter? What use is a gold coin to him? It can't be eaten or planted. 'Tis good only when given to others."

Both Quinton and Palgrave dropped their shoulders, folded in their arms, and looked downward in guilt.

Warwick sighed. His face looked worn and fatigued, and shadows played across his features. "Forgive me, men. Let me steal your minds from this misery by a tale of a hard lesson learned."

Adam McFarlane's writing appears in *Sherlock Holmes Mystery Magazine*, *Thuglit*, and *Mid-Century Murder* (forthcoming). He lives in Minnesota.

Quinton and Palgrave pulled their chairs closer. Other patrons paused to listen.

"Look at this." Warwick pulled off his glove, and he showed us his hand. It was small, nearly dainty. The skin was white and smooth.

"Aye," I said with Quinton and Palgrave.

He put both hands together. The other looked enormous, hairy and rough, with skin so tanned and dried it was nearly leather. "I was born with but one hand, so one arm was a useless stump." He clenched his smaller hand into a fist. "I was my family's shame."

"Ashamed o' the way you was born?" Quinton shook his head. "That's nowise fair."

With a slow nod, Warwick agreed. "People imagine the worst about what they don't understand. The priest banned me from church. Christ, he said, healed the sick and the crippled just as he drove away demons. As God did not give me a good hand, I belonged in a church inasmuch as a man possessed."

As far as I could tell, his smaller hand looked real.

Warwick went on. "I joined a pirate crew, where I felt welcome and normal, and I learned to use a hook for a hand."

I tried to imagine him younger, the wrinkles starched from his face and the gray dyed out of his hair, clean-shaven, in trousers and white shirtsleeves. Standing on the bow of a frigate, he let the spray of waves cool the equatorial heat as he cut across the ocean.

"I raided every port between Good Hope and the Dutch East Indies. I made so many enemies, I needed a safe harbor to hide. Such a place was Tascara, capital of Arabia. Its sultan ruled from Zanzibar to Muscat. Crowned by a gold dome, the palace's horseshoe-shaped arches opened to a courtyard. Its stone floor was a mosaic swirl of green and red tiles.

"The sultan was Pasha Ahmed Seydi Hasan. His hair, beard, and eyes were black as coal, but time had carved deep grooves into his face. Rumors were that Pasha Hasan was one hundred years old, but he used magic to become a younger man. Swaddled in silk from turban to slippers, he sat on a throne of ivory and ebony. Creating a gentle breeze, slaves waved large fans. Embroidered curtains hid the entrance to his harem."

"'Harem?'" I asked.

"A stable of wives," Quinton explained.

"Ohhh," I exclaimed as my mind bent around the idea.

Warwick continued. "Yes, and they lounged on tasseled velvet pillows in the courtyard. Each wore loose-fitting pants that bloomed at their ankles. Clothing dotted with gold barely covered their bosoms — *brassieres*, be the word. When they walked, tiny anklet bells jingled."

Palgrave and Quinton exhaled in amazement.

"He maintained a score of slaves, weak in body and mind. They were eunuchs, having had their manhood taken away, and kept barely fed."

"I cannot imagine being so rich and powerful as to have slaves and everything I could ever dream of," I said.

"The sultan had *almost* everything." A

sly smile crept into the corner of Warwick's mouth.

"What more could he want?" I asked.

"I offered him a teleportation spell that enabled whole ships to travel fifty miles in the blink of an eye."

"As pirates have long used them to escape navies, such spells are extremely expensive," Palgrave said. "But why would a sultan want a teleportation spell?"

Warwick responded. "When I heard about Blackbeard using one to cross Guatemala from the Atlantic to the Pacific, I realized they could be useful for merchants. This is how I explained it to the sultan." He raised a finger. "If he possessed the spell, his ships could sail from Kolzum to Port Said."

I pictured a map in my head — one was on the Red Sea, one in the Mediterranean, separated by a triangle of Egypt.

"If such spells exist, then why don't we use them all the time? Why sail across the ocean when we could skip across it magically?" Quinton asked.

"The tools to cast such a spell are costly," Warwick said. "The blood of a goat must be spilled as the scroll of the spell is burned, all the while reciting the spell aloud. It's too much for a pirate ship to do often in one voyage. But for a merchant ship, it is nothing for the spell to be cast on shore while the ship passes nearby. Without sailing around Africa or portaging over Sinai, the sultan could deliver cargo into Christendom in half the time."

"Brilliant, Captain," Palgrave said.

"What did he pay you in return?" Quinton asked.

"Heed this part, lads, for this is why I chose Tascara over Libertalia or Blackport. 'It is said that you have the power to heal wounds beyond repair,' I said and showed him my arm."

I topped off the captain's glass, as well as Quinton's and Palgrave's, keeping their cups full and hot.

"And thus, the bargain was struck. When the magic rite began, the court wizard recited an incantation, a cleric muttered a prayer for God's blessing, and a slave was prepared for sacrifice."

Warwick stopped and looked hard at us. "Sacrifice, men. A eunuch laid down his arm while a guard sharpened an axe. The sultan could *not* grow me a hand. He intended to put the slave's hand onto my arm."

A shiver wriggled inside me.

"I'd not stand for a sacrifice on my account," he said. "So, I cried out for the wizard to stop. It is a deadly thing, ceasing a spell before its casting. But I could not take the hand of another and leave it with the fate I had.

"The sultan laughed. 'Do you not want a hand? What else do you desire? Women? Riches? Magic?'

"Dumbstruck, I had nothing to want, nothing else I had sailed there for.

"He laughed again. 'Foolish, Christian. Perhaps if I filled your glove with pearls to offer as payment, that would suffice?'

"In addition to the slave's hand?" Quinton asked. "To persuade you to take it?"

Warwick shook his head. "To the slave whose hand would be sacrificed, as if the sultan were buying the hand. Not *taking* then, but *purchasing* at fair bargain."

(Continued on page 100)

BREATH OF ALLAH

BY SAX ROHMER

I

FOR close upon a week I had been haunting the purlieus of the Mûski, attired as a respectable dragoman, my face and hands reduced to a deeper shade of brown by means of a water-color paint (I had to use something that could be washed off and grease-paint is useless for purposes of actual disguise) and a neat black moustache fixed to my lip with spirit-gum. In his story *Beyond the Pale*, Rudyard Kipling has trounced the man who inquires too deeply into native life; but if everybody thought with Kipling we should never have

had a Lane or a Burton and I should have continued in unbroken scepticism regarding the reality of magic. Whereas, because of the matters which I am about to set forth, for ten minutes of my life I found myself a trembling slave of the unknown.

Let me explain at once that my undignified masquerade was not prompted by mere curiosity or the quest of the pomegranate, it was undertaken as the natural sequel to a letter received from Messrs. Moses, Murphy and Co., the firm which I represented in Egypt, containing curious matters affording much food for reflection. "We would ask you," ran the communication, "to renew your inquiries into the particular composition of the perfume 'Breath of Allah,' of which you obtained us a sample at a cost which we regarded as excessive. It appears to consist in the blending of certain obscure essential oils and gum-resins; and the nature of some of these has defied analysis to date. Over a hundred experiments have been made to discover substitutes for the missing essences, but without success; and as we are now in a position to arrange for the manufacture of Oriental perfume on an extensive scale we should be prepared to make it *well worth your while* (the last four words character-istically underlined in red ink) if you could obtain for us a correct copy of the original prescription."

The letter went on to say that it was proposed to establish a separate company for the exploitation of the new perfume, with a registered address in Cairo and a "manufactory" in some suitably inaccessible spot in the Near East.

I pondered deeply over these matters. The scheme was a good one and could not fail to reap considerable profits; for, given extensive advertising, there is always a large and monied public for a new smell. The particular blend of liquid fragrance to which the letter referred was assured of a good sale at a high price, not alone in Egypt, but throughout the capitals of the world, provided it could be put upon the market; but the proposition of manufacture was beset with extraordinary difficulties.

The tiny vial I despatched to Birmingham nearly twelve months before had cost me close upon £100 to procure, for the reason that "Breath of Allah" was the secret property of an old and aristocratic Egyptian family whose great wealth and exclusiveness rendered them unapproachable. By dint of diligent inquiry I had discovered the *attár* to whom was entrusted certain final processes in the preparation of the perfume — only to learn he was ignorant of its exact composition. Although he had assured me (and I did not doubt his word) that not one grain had hitherto passed out of the possession of the family, I had succeeded in procuring a small quantity of the precious fluid.

Messrs. Moses, Murphy and Co. had made all the necessary arrangements for placing it upon the market, only to learn, as this eventful letter advised me, that the most skilled chemists whose services were obtainable had failed to analyze it.

One morning, then, in my assumed character, I was proceeding along the Shâria el-Hamzâwi seeking for some scheme whereby I might win the confidence of Mohammed er-Rahmân the *attár*, or perfumer. I had quitted the house in the Darb el-Ahmar which was my base of operations but a few minutes earlier, and as I approached

Arthur Henry "Sarsfield" Ward, better known as **Sax Rohmer,** was a prolific English novelist. He is best remembered for his series of novels featuring the master criminal Dr. Fu Manchu. "Breath of Allah" originally appeared in *The Premier Magazine,* February 1917.

the corner of the street a voice called from a window directly above my head: "Saïd! Saïd!"

Without supposing the call referred to myself, I glanced up, and met the gaze of an old Egyptian of respectable appearance who was regarding me from above. Shading his eyes with a gnarled hand —

"Surely," he cried, "it is none other than Saïd the nephew of Yûssuf Khalig! *Es-selâm 'aleykûm, Saïd!*"

"*Aleykûm, es-selâm,*" I replied, and stood there looking up at him.

"Would you perform a little service for me, Saïd?" he continued. "It will occupy you but an hour and you may earn five piastres."

"Willingly," I replied, not knowing to what the mistake of this evidently half-blind old man might lead me.

I entered the door and mounted the stairs to the room in which he was, to find that he lay upon a scantily covered divan by the open window.

"Praise be to Allah (whose name be exalted)!" he exclaimed, "that I am thus fortunately enabled to fulfil my obligations. I sometimes suffer from an old serpent bite, my son, and this morning it has obliged me to abstain from all movement. I am called Abdûl the Porter, of whom you will have heard your uncle speak; and although I have long retired from active labor myself, I contract for the supply of porters and carriers of all descriptions and for all purposes; conveying fair ladies to the *hammám*, youth to the bridal, and death to the grave. Now, it was written that you should arrive at this timely hour."

I considered it highly probable that it was also written how I should shortly depart if this garrulous old man continued to inflict upon me details of his absurd career. However —

"I have a contract with the merchant, Mohammed er-Rahmân of the Sûk el-Attârin," he continued, "which it has always been my custom personally to carry out."

The words almost caused me to catch my breath; and my opinion of Abdul the Porter changed extraordinary. Truly my lucky star had guided my footsteps that morning!

"Do not misunderstand me," he added. "I refer not to the transport of his wares to Suez, to Zagazig, to Mecca, to Aleppo, to Baghdad, Damascus, Kandahar, and Pekin; although the whole of these vast enterprises is entrusted to none other than the only son of my father: I speak, now, of the bearing of a small though heavy box from the great magazine and manufactory of Mohammed er-Rahmân at Shubra, to his shop in the Sûk el-Attârin, a matter which I have arranged for him on the eve of the Molid en-Nebi — birthday of the Prophet — for the past five-and-thirty years. Every one of my porters to whom I might entrust this special charge is otherwise employed; hence my observation that it was written how none other than yourself should pass beneath this window at a certain fortunate hour."

Fortunate indeed had that hour been for me, and my pulse beat far from normally as I put the question: "Why, O Father Abdul, do you attach so much importance to this seemingly trivial matter?"

The face of Abdul the Porter, which resembled that of an intelligent mule, assumed an expression of low cunning.

"The question is well conceived," he said, raising a long forefinger and wagging it at me. "And who in all Cairo knows so much of the secrets of the great as Abdul the Know-all, Abdul the Taciturn! Ask me of the fabled wealth of Karafa Bey and I will name you every one of his possessions and entertain you with a calculation of his income, which I have worked out in *nûss-faddah*!

"Ask me of the amber mole upon the shoulder of the Princess Azîza and I will describe it to you in such a manner as to ravish your soul! Whisper, my son" — he bent towards me confidentially — "once a year the merchant Mohammed er-Rahmân prepares for the Lady Zuleyka a quantity of the perfume which impious tradition has called 'Breath of Allah.' The father of Mohammed er-Rahmân prepared it for the mother of the Lady Zuleyka and his father before him for the lady of that day who held the secret — the secret which has belonged to the women of this family since the reign of the Khalîf el-Hakîm from whose favorite wife they are descended. To her, the wife of the Khalîf, the first *dirhem* ever distilled of the perfume was presented in a gold vase, together with the manner of its preparation, by the great wizard and physician Ibn Sina of Bokhara."

"You are well called Abdul the Know-all!" I cried in admiration. "Then the secret is held by Mohammed er-Rahmân?"

"Not so, my son," replied Abdul. "Certain of the essences employed are brought, in sealed vessels, from the house of the Lady Zuleyka, as is also the brass coffer containing the writing of Ibn Sina; and throughout the measuring of the quantities, the secret writing never leaves her hand."

"What, the Lady Zuelyka attends in person?"

Abdul the Porter inclined his head serenely.

"On the eve of the birthday of the Prophet, the Lady Zuelyka visits the shop of Mohammed er-Rahmân, accompanied by an *imám* from one of the great mosques."

"Why by an *imám*, Father Abdul?"

"There is a magical ritual which must be observed in the distillation of the perfume, and each essence is blessed in the name of one of the four archangels; and the whole operation must commence at the hour of midnight on the eve of the Molid en-Nebi."

He peered at me triumphantly.

"Surely," I protested, "an experienced *attár* such as Mohammed er-Rahmân would readily recognize these secret ingredients by their smell?"

"A great pan of burning charcoal," whispered Abdul dramatically, "is placed upon the floor of the room, and throughout the operation the attendant *imám* casts pungent spices upon it, whereby the nature of the secret essences is rendered unrecognizable. It is time you depart, my son, to the shop of Mohammed, and I will give you a writing making you known to him. Your task will be to carry the materials necessary for the secret operation (which takes place to-night) from the magazine of Mohammed er-Rahmân at Shubra, to his shop in the Sûk el-Attârin. My eyesight is far from good, Saïd. Do you write as I direct and I will place my name to the letter?"

II

The words "well worth your while" had kept time to my steps, or I doubt if I should have survived the odious journey from Shubra. Never can I forget the shape, color, and especially the weight, of the locked chest which was my burden. Old Mohammed er-Rahmân had accepted my service on the strength of the letter signed by Abdul, and of course, had failed to recognize in "Saïd" that Hon. Neville Kernaby who had certain confidential dealings with him a year before. But exactly how I was to profit by the fortunate accident which had led Abdul to mistake me for someone called "Saïd" became more and more obscure as the box grew more and more heavy. So that by the time that I actually arrived with my burden at the entrance to the Street of the Perfumers, my heart had hardened towards Abdul the Know-all; and, setting my box upon the ground, I seated myself upon it to rest and to imprecate at leisure that silent cause of my present exhaustion.

After a time, my troubled spirit grew calmer, as I sat there inhaling the insidious breath of Tonquin musk, the fragrance of attár of roses, the sweetness of Indian spike-nard and the stinging pungency of myrrh, opoponax, and ihlang-ylang. Faintly I could detect the perfume which I have always counted the most exquisite of all save one — that delightful preparation of Jasmine peculiarly Egyptian. But the mystic breath of frankincense and erotic fumes of amber-gris alike left me unmoved; for amid these odors, through which it has always seemed to me that that of cedar runs thematically, I sought in vain for any hint of "Breath of Allah."

Fashionable Europe and America were well represented as usual in the Sûk el-Attârin, but the little shop of Mohammed er-Rahmân was quite deserted, although he dealt in the most rare essences of all. Mohammed, however, did not seek Western patronage, nor was there in the heart of the little white-bearded merchant any envy of his seemingly more prosperous neighbors in whose shops New York, London, and Paris smoked amber-scented cigarettes, and whose wares were carried to the uttermost corners of the earth.

There is nothing more illusory than the outward seeming of the Eastern merchant. The wealthiest man with whom I was acquainted in the Muski had the aspect of a mendicant; and whilst Mohammed's neighbors sold phials of essence and tiny boxes of pastilles to the patrons of Messrs. Cook, were not the silent caravans following the ancient desert routes laden with great crates of sweet merchandise from the manufactory at Shubra? To the city of Mecca alone Mohammed sent annually perfumes to the value of two thousand pounds sterling; he manufactured three kinds of incense exclusively for the royal house of Persia; and his wares were known from Alexandria to Kashmîr, and prized alike in Stambûl and Tartary. Well might he watch with tolerant smile the more showy activities of his less fortunate competitors.

The shop of Mohammed er-Rahmân was at the end of the street remote from the Hamzâwi (Cloth Bazaar), and as I stood up to resume my labors my mood of gloomy abstraction was changed as much by a certain atmosphere of expectancy — I cannot otherwise describe it — as by the familiar smells of the place. I had taken no more than three paces onward into the Sûk ere it seemed to me that all business had suddenly become suspended; only the Western element of the throng remained outside whatever influence had claimed the Orientals. Then presently the visitors, also becoming aware of this expectant hush as I had become aware of it, turned almost with one accord, and following the direction of the merchants' glances, gazed up the narrow street towards the Mosque of el-Ashraf.

And here I must chronicle a curious circumstance. Of the Imám Abû Tabâh I had seen nothing for several weeks, but at this moment I suddenly found myself thinking of that remarkable man. Whilst any mention of his name, or nickname — for I could not believe "Tabâh" to be patronymic — amongst the natives led only to pious ejaculations indicative of respectful fear, by the official world he was tacitly disowned. Yet I had indisputable evidence to show that few doors in Cairo, or indeed in all Egypt, were124 closed to him; he came and went like a phantom. I should never have been surprised, on entering my private apartments at Shepheard's, to have found him seated therein, nor did I question the veracity of a native acquaintance who assured me that he had met the mysterious imám in Aleppo on the same morning that a letter from his partner in Cairo had arrived mentioning a visit by Abû Tabâh to el-Azhar. But throughout the native city he was known as the Magician and was very generally regarded as a master of the ginn. Once more depositing my burden upon the ground, then, I gazed with the rest in the direction of the mosque.

It was curious, that moment of perfumed silence, and my imagination, doubtless inspired by the memory of Abû Tabâh, was carried back to the days of the great khalîfs, which never seem far removed from one in those mediæval streets. I was transported to the Cairo of Harûn al Raschîd, and I thought that the Grand Wazîr on some mission from Baghdad was visiting the Sûk el-Attârin.

Then, stately through the silent group, came a black-robed, white-turbaned figure outwardly similar to many others in the bazaar, but followed by two tall muffled negroes. So still was the place that I could hear the tap of his ebony stick as he strode along the center of the street.

At the shop of Mohammed er-Rahmân he paused, exchanging a few words with the merchant, then resumed his way, coming down the Sûk towards me. His glance met mine, as I stood there beside the box; and, to my amazement, he saluted me with smiling dignity and passed on. Had he, too, mistaken me for Saïd — or had his all-seeing gaze detected beneath my disguise the features of Neville Kernaby?

As he turned out of the narrow street into the Hamzâwi, the commercial uproar was resumed instantly, so that save for this horrible doubt which had set my heart beating with uncomfortable rapidity, by all the evidences now about me his coming might have been a dream.

III

Filled with misgivings, I carried the box along to the shop; but Mohammed er Rahmân's greeting held no hint of suspicion.

"By fleetness of foot thou shalt never win Paradise," he said.

"Nor by unseemly haste shall I thrust others from the path," I retorted.

"It is idle to bandy words with any acquaintance of Abdul the Porter's," sighed Mohammed; "well do I know it. Take up the box and follow me."

With a key which he carried attached to a chain about his waist, he unlocked the ancient door which alone divided his shop from the out-jutting wall marking a bend in the street. A native shop is usually nothing more than a double cell; but descending three stone steps, I found myself in one of those cellar-like apartments which are not uncommon in this part of Cairo. Windows there were none, if I except a small square opening, high up in one of the walls, which evidently communicated with the narrow courtyard separating Mohammed's establishment from that of his neighbor, but which admitted scanty light and less ventilation. Through this opening I could see what looked like the uplifted shafts of a cart. From one of the rough beams of the rather lofty ceiling a brass lamp hung by chains, and a quantity of primitive chemical paraphernalia littered the place; old-fashioned alembics, mysterious looking jars, and a sort of portable furnace, together with several tripods and a number of large, flat brass pans gave the place the appearance of some old alchemist's den. A rather

handsome ebony table, intricately carved and inlaid with mother-o'-pearl and ivory, stood before a cushioned *dîwan* which occupied that side of the room in which was the square window.

"Set the box upon the floor," directed Mohammed, "but not with such undue dispatch as to cause thyself to sustain an injury."

That he had been eagerly awaiting the arrival of the box and was now burningly anxious to witness my departure, grew more and more apparent with every word. Therefore —

"There are asses who are fleet of foot," I said, leisurely depositing my load at his feet; "but the wise man regulateth his pace in accordance with three things: the heat of the sun; the welfare of others; and the nature of his burden."

"That thou hast frequently paused on the way127 from Shubra to reflect upon these three things," replied Mohammed, "I cannot doubt; depart, therefore, and ponder them at leisure, for I perceive that thou art a great philosopher."

"Philosophy," I continued, seating myself upon the box, "sustaineth the mind, but the activity of the mind being dependent upon the welfare of the stomach, even the philosopher cannot afford to labor without hire."

At that, Mohammed er-Rahmân unloosed upon me a long pent-up torrent of invective — and furnished me with the information which I was seeking.

"O son of a wall-eyed mule!" he cried, shaking his fists over me, "no longer will I suffer thy idiotic chatter! Return to Abdul the Porter, who employed thee, for not one *faddah* will I give thee, calamitous mongrel that thou art! Depart! for I was but this moment informed that a lady of high station is about to visit me. Depart! lest she mistake my shop for a pigsty."

But even as he spoke the words, I became aware of a vague disturbance in the street, and —

"Ah!" cried Mohammed, running to the foot of the steps and gazing upwards, "now am I utterly undone! Shame of thy parents that thou art, it is now unavoidable that the Lady Zuleyka shall find thee in my shop. Listen, offensive insect — thou art Saïd, my assistant. Utter not one word; or with this" — to my great alarm he produced a dangerous-looking pistol from beneath his robe — "will I blow a hole through thy vacuous skull!"

Hastily concealing the pistol, he went hurrying up the steps, in time to perform a low salutation before a veiled woman who was accompanied by a Sûdanese servant-girl and a negro. Exchanging some words with her which I was unable to detect, Mohammed er-Rahmân led the way down into the apartment wherein I stood, followed by the lady, who in turn was followed by her servant. The negro remained above. Perceiving me as she entered, the lady, who was attired with extraordinary elegance, paused, glancing at Mohammed.

"My lady," he began immediately, bowing before her, "it is Saïd my assistant, the slothfulness of whose habits is only exceeded by the impudence of his conversation."

She hesitated, bestowing upon me a glance of her beautiful eyes. Despite the gloom of the place and the *yashmak* which she wore, it was manifest that she was good to look upon. A faint but exquisite perfume stole to my nostrils, whereby I knew that Mohammed's charming visitor was none other than, the Lady Zuleyka.

"Yet," she said softly, "he hath the look of an active young man."

"His activity," replied the scent merchant, "resideth entirely in his tongue."

The Lady Zuleyka seated herself upon the *dîwan*, looking all about the apartment.

"Everything is in readiness, Mohammed?" she asked.

"Everything, my lady."

Again the beautiful eyes were turned in my direction, and, as their inscrutable gaze rested upon me, a scheme — which, since it was never carried out, need not be described — presented itself to my mind. Following a brief but eloquent silence — for my answering glances were laden with significance: —

"O Mohammed," said the Lady Zuleyka indolently, "in what manner doth a merchant, such as thyself, chastise his servants when their conduct displeaseth him?"

Mohammed er-Rahmân seemed somewhat at a loss for a reply, and stood there staring foolishly.

"I have whips for mine," murmured the soft voice. "It is an old custom of my family."

Slowly she cast her eyes in my direction once more.

"It seemed to me, O Saïd," she continued, gracefully resting one jeweled hand upon the ebony table, "that thou hadst presumed to cast love-glances upon me. There is one waiting above whose duty it is to protect me from such insults. Miska!" — to the servant girl — "summon El-Kimri (The Dove)."

Whilst I stood there dumbfounded and abashed the girl called up the steps:

"El-Kimri! Come hither!"

Instantly there burst into the room the form of that hideous negro whom I had glimpsed above; and —

"O Kimri," directed the Lady Zuleyka, and languidly extended her hand in my direction, "throw this presumptuous clown into the street!"

My discomfiture had proceeded far enough, and I recognized that, at whatever risk of discovery, I must act instantly. Therefore, at the moment that El-Kimri reached the foot of the steps, I dashed my left fist into his grinning face, putting all my weight behind the blow, which I followed up with a short right, utterly outraging the pugilistic proprieties, since it was well below the belt. El-Kimri bit the dust to the accompaniment of a human discord composed of three notes—and I leaped up the steps, turned to the left, and ran off around the Mosque of el-Ashraf, where I speedily lost myself in the crowded Ghurîya.

Beneath their factitious duskiness my cheeks were burning hotly: I was ashamed of my execrable artistry. For a druggist's assistant does not lightly make love to a duchess!

IV

I spent the remainder of the forenoon at my house in the Darb el-Ahmar heaping curses upon my own fatuity and upon the venerable head of Abdul the Know-all. At one moment it seemed to me that I had wantonly destroyed a golden opportunity, at the next that the seeming opportunity had been a mere mirage. With the passing of noon and the approach of evening I sought desperately for a plan, knowing that if I failed to conceive one by midnight, another chance of seeing the famous prescription would probably not present itself for twelve months.

At about four o'clock in the afternoon came the dawn of a hazy idea, and since it necessitated a visit to my rooms at Shepheard's, I washed the paint off my face and hands, changed, hurried to the hotel, ate a hasty meal, and returned to the Darb el-Ahmar, where I resumed my disguise.

There are some who have criticized me harshly in regard to my commercial activities at this time, and none of my affairs has provoked greater acerbitude than that of the perfume called "Breath of Allah." Yet I am at a loss to perceive wherein my perfidy lay; for my outlook is sufficiently socialistic to cause me to regard with displeasure the conserving by an individual of something which, without loss to himself, might reasonably be shared by the community. For this reason, I have always resented the way in which the Moslem veils the faces of the pearls of his *harêm*. And whilst the success of my present enterprise would not render the Lady Zuleyka the poorer, it would enrich and beautify the world by delighting the senses of men with a perfume more exquisite than any hitherto known.

Such were my reflections as I made my way through the dark and deserted bazaar quarter, following the Shâria el-Akkadi to the Mosque of el-Ashraf. There I turned to the left in the direction of the Hamzâwi, until, coming to the narrow alley opening from it into the Sûk el-Attârin, I plunged into its darkness, which was like that of a tunnel, although the upper parts of the houses above were silvered by the moon.

I was making for that cramped little courtyard adjoining the shop of Mohammed er-Rahmân in which I had observed the presence of one of those narrow high-wheeled carts peculiar to the district, and as the entrance thereto from the Sûk was closed by a rough wooden fence I antici-pated little difficult in gaining access. Yet there was one difficulty which I had not foreseen, and which I had not met with had I arrived, as I might easily have arranged to do, a little earlier. Coming to the corner of the Street of the Perfumers, I cautiously protruded my head in order to survey the prospect.

Abû Tabâh was standing immediately outside the shop of Mohammed er-Rah-mân!

My heart gave a great leap as I drew back into the shadow, for I counted his presence of evil omen to the success of my enterprise. Then, a swift revelation, the truth burst in upon my mind. He was there in the capacity of *imám* and attendant magi-cian at the mystical "Blessing of the per-fumes"! With cautious tread I retraced my steps, circled round the Mosque and made for the narrow street which runs parallel with that of the Perfumers and into which I knew the courtyard beside Mohammed's shop must open. What I did not know was how I was going to enter it from that end.

I experienced unexpected difficulty in locating the place, for the height of the buildings about me rendered it impossible to pick up any familiar landmark. Finally, having twice retraced my steps, I deter-mined that a door of old but strong work-man133ship set in a high, thick wall must communicate with the courtyard; for I could see no other opening to the right, or left through which it would have been possible for a vehicle to pass.

Mechanically I tried the door, but, as I had anticipated, found it to be securely locked. A profound silence reigned all about me and there was no window in sight from which my operations could be observed. Therefore, having planned out my route, I determined to scale the wall. My first foot-hold was offered by the heavy wooden lock which projected fully six inches from the door. Above it was a crossbeam and then a gap of several inches between the top of the gate and the arch into which it was built. Above the arch projected an iron rod from which depended a hook; and if I could reach the bar it would be possible to get astride the wall.

I reached the bar successfully, and although it proved to be none too firmly fastened, I took the chance and without making very much noise found myself perched aloft and looking down into the little court. A sigh of relief escaped me; for the narrow cart with its disproportionate wheels stood there as I had seen it in the morning, its shafts pointing gauntly upward to where the moon of the Prophet's nativity swam in a cloudless sky. A dim light shone out from the square window of Mohammed er-Rahmân's cellar.

Having studied the situation very care-fully, I presently perceived to my great satisfaction that whilst the tail of the cart was wedged under a crossbar, which retained it in its position, one of the shafts was in reach of my hand. Thereupon I entrusted my weight to the shaft, swinging out over the well of the courtyard. So successful was I that only a faint creaking sound resulted; and I descended into the vehicle almost silently.

Having assured myself that my presence was undiscovered by Abû Tabâh, I stood up cautiously, my hands resting upon the wall, and peered through the little window into the room. Its appearance had changed somewhat. The lamp was lighted and shed a weird and subdued illumination upon a rough table placed almost beneath it. Upon this table were scales, measures, curiously shaped flasks, and odd-looking chemical apparatus which might have been made in the days of Avicenna himself. At one end of the table stood an alembic over a little pan in which burnt a spirituous flame. Mohammed er-Rahmân was placing cushions upon the *dîwan* immediately beneath me, but there was no one else in the room. Glancing upward, I noted that the height of the neighboring building prevented the moonlight from penetrating into the courtyard, so that my presence could not be detected by means of any light from without; and, since the whole of the upper part of the room was shadowed, I saw little cause for apprehension within.

At this moment came the sound of a car approaching along the Shâria esh-Sharawâni. I heard it stop, near the Mosque of el-Ashraf, and in the almost perfect stillness of those tortuous streets from which by day arises a very babel of tongues I heard approaching footsteps. I crouched down in the cart, as the footsteps came nearer, passed the end of the courtyard abutting on the Street of the Perfumers, and paused before the shop of Mohammed er-Rahmân. The musical voice of Abû Tabâh spoke and that of the Lady Zuleyka answered. Came a loud rapping, and the creak of an opening door: then —

"Descend the steps, place the coffer on the table, and then remain immediately outside the door," continued the imperious voice of the lady. "Make sure that there are no eavesdroppers."

Faintly through the little window there reached my ears a sound as of some heavy object being placed upon a wooden surface, then a muffled disturbance as of several persons entering the room; finally, the muffled bang of a door closed and barred ... and soft footsteps in the adjoining street!

Crouching down in the cart and almost holding my breath, I watched through a hole in the side of the ramshackle vehicle that fence to which I have already referred as closing the end of the courtyard which adjoined the Sûk el-Attârin. A spear of moonlight, penetrating through some gap in the surrounding buildings, silvered its extreme edge. To an accompaniment of much kicking and heavy breathing, into this natural limelight arose the black countenance of "The Dove." To my unbounded joy I perceived that his nose was lavishly decorated with sticking-plaster and that his right eye was temporarily off duty. Eight fat fingers clutching at the top of the woodwork, the bloated negro regarded the apparently empty yard for a space of some three seconds, ere lowering his ungainly bulk to the level of the street again. Followed a faint "pop" and a gurgling quite unmistakable. I heard him walking back to the door, as I cautiously stood up and again surveyed the interior of the room.

V

Egypt, as the earliest historical records show, has always been a land of magic, and according to native belief it is to-day the theater of many super-natural dramas. For my own part, prior to the episode which I am about to relate, my personal experiences of the kind had been limited and unconvincing. That Abû Tabâh possessed a sort of uncanny power akin to second sight I knew, but I regarded it merely as a form of telepathy. His presence at the preparation of the secret perfume did not surprise me, for a belief in the efficacy of magical operations prevailed, as I was aware, even among the more cultured Moslems. My skepticism, however, was about to be rudely shaken.

As I raised my head above the ledge of the window and looked into the room, I perceived the Lady Zuleyka seated on the cushioned *divan*, her hands resting upon an open roll of parchment which lay upon the table beside a massive brass chest of antique native workmanship. The lid of the chest was raised, and the interior seemed to be empty, but near it upon the table I observed a number of gold-stoppered vessels of Venetian glass and each of which was of a different color.

Beside a brazier wherein glowed a charcoal fire, Abû Tabâh stood; and into the fire he cast alternately strips of paper bearing writing of some sort and little dark brown pastilles which he took from a sandalwood box set upon a sort of tripod beside him. They were composed of some kind of aromatic gum in which benzoin seemed to predominate, and the fumes from the brazier filled the room with a blue mist.

The *imám*, in his soft, musical voice, was reciting that chapter of the Korân called "The Angel." The weird ceremony had begun. In order to achieve my purpose, I perceived that I should have to draw myself right up to the narrow embrasure and rest my weight entirely upon the ledge of the window. There was little danger in the maneuver, provided I made no noise; for the hanging lamp, by reason of its form, cast no light into the upper part of the room. As I achieved the desired position, I became painfully aware of the pungency of the perfume with which the apartment was filled.

Lying there upon the ledge in a most painful attitude, I wriggled forward inch by inch further into the room, until I was in a position to use my right arm more or less freely. The preliminary prayer concluded, the measuring of the perfumes had now actually commenced, and I readily perceived that without recourse to the parchment, from which the Lady Zuleyka never once removed her hands, it would indeed be impossible to discover the secret. For, consulting the ancient prescription, she would select one of the gold-stoppered bottles, unscrew it, direct that so many grains should be taken from it, and never removing her gaze from Mohammed er-Rahmân whilst he measured out the correct quantity, would restopper the vessel and so proceed. As each was placed in a wide-mouthed glass jar by the perfumer, Abû Tabâh, extending his hands over the jar, pronounced the names:

"Gabraîl Mikaîl, Israfîl, Israîl."

Cautiously I raised to my eyes the small but powerful opera-glasses to procure which I had gone to my rooms at Shepheard's. Focusing them upon the ancient scroll lying on the table beneath me, I discovered, to my joy, that I could read the lettering quite well. Whilst Abû Tabâh began to recite some kind of incantation in the course of which the names of the Companions of the Prophet frequently occurred, I commenced to read the writing of Avicenna.

"In the name of God, the Compassionate, the Merciful, the High, the Great ...."

So far had I proceeded and no further when I became aware of a curious change in the form of the Arabic letters. They seemed to be moving, to be cunningly changing places one with another as if to trick me out of grasping their meaning!

The illusion persisting, I determined that it was due to the unnatural strain imposed upon my vision, and although I recognized that time was precious I found myself compelled temporarily to desist, since nothing was to be gained by watching these letters which danced from side to side of the parchment, sometimes in groups and sometimes singly, so that I found myself pursuing one slim Arab A ('Alif) entirely up the page from the bottom to the top where it finally disappeared under the thumb of the Lady Zuleyka!

Lowering the glasses, I stared down in stupefaction at Abû Tabâh. He had just cast fresh incense upon the flames, and it came home to me, with a childish

and unreasoning sense of terror, that the Egyptians who called this man the Magician were wiser than I. For whilst I could no longer hear his voice, I now could *see* the words issuing from his mouth! They formed slowly and gracefully in the blue clouds of vapour some four feet above his head, revealed their meaning to me in letters of gold, and then faded away towards the ceiling!

Old-established beliefs began to totter about me as I became aware of a number of small murmuring voices within the room. They were the voices of the perfumes burning in the brazier. Said one, in a guttural tone:

"I am Myrrh. My voice is the voice of the Tomb."

And another softly: "I am Ambergris. I lure the hearts of men."

And a third huskily: "I am Patchouli. My promises are lies."

My sense of smell seemed to have deserted me and to have been replaced by a sense of hearing. And now this room of magic began to expand before my eyes. The walls receded and receded, until the apartment grew larger than the interior of the Citadel Mosque; the roof shot up so high that I knew there was no cathedral in the world half so lofty. Abû Tabâh, his hands extended above the brazier, shrank to minute dimensions, and the Lady Zuleyka, seated beneath me, became almost invisible.

The project which had led me to thrust myself into the midst of this feast of sorcery vanished from my mind. I desired but one thing: to depart, ere reason utterly deserted me. But, to my horror, I discovered that my muscles were become rigid bands of iron! The figure of Abû Tabâh was drawing nearer; his slowly moving arms had grown serpentine and his eyes had changed to pools of flame which seemed to summon me. At the time when this new phenomenon added itself to the other horrors, I seemed to be impelled by an irresistible force to jerk my head downwards: I heard my neck muscles snap metallically: I *saw* a scream of agony spurt forth from my lips ... and I saw upon a little ledge immediately below the square window a little *mibkharah*, or incense burner, which hitherto I had not observed. A thick, oily brown stream of vapor was issuing from its perforated lid and bathing my face clammily. Sense of smell I had none; but a chuckling, demoniacal voice spoke from the *mibkharah*, saying —

"I am *Hashish*! I drive men mad! Whilst thou hast lain up there like a very fool, I have sent my vapors to thy brain and stolen thy senses from thee. It was for this purpose that I was set here beneath the window where thou couldst not fail to enjoy the full benefit of my poisonous perfume ...."

Slipping off the ledge, I fell ... and darkness closed about me.

VI

My awakening constitutes one of the most painful recollections of a not uneventful career, for, with aching head and tortured limbs, I sat upright upon the floor of a tiny, stuffy, and uncleanly cell! The only light was that which entered by way of a little grating in the door. I was a prisoner; and, in the same instant that I realized the fact of my incarceration, I realized also that I had been duped. The weird happenings in

the apartment of Mohammed er-Rahmân had been hallucinations due to my having inhaled the fumes of some preparation of *hashish*, or Indian hemp. The characteristic sickly odor of the drug had been concealed by the pungency of the other and more odoriferous perfumes; and because of the position of the censer containing the burning *hashish*, no one else in the room had been affected by its vapor. Could it have been that Abû Tabâh had known of my presence from the first?

I rose, unsteadily, and looked out through the grating into a narrow passage. A native constable stood at one end of it, and beyond him I obtained a glimpse of the entrance hall. Instantly I recognized that I was under arrest at the Bâb el-Khalk police station!

A great rage consumed me. Raising my fists, I banged furiously upon the door, and the Egyptian policeman came running along the passage.

"What does this mean, *shawêsh*?" I demanded. "Why am I detained here? I am an Englishman. Send the superintendent to me instantly."

The policeman's face expressed alternately anger, surprise, and stupefaction.

"You were brought here last night, most disgustingly and speechlessly drunk, in a cart!" he replied.

"I demand to see the superintendent."

"Certainly, certainly, *effendim*!" cried the man, now thoroughly alarmed. "In an instant, *effendim*!"

Such is the magical power of the word "Inglîsi" (Englishman).

A painfully perturbed and apologetic native official appeared almost immediately, to whom I explained that I had been to a fancy-dress ball at the Gezira Palace Hotel, and, injudiciously walking homeward at a late hour, had been attacked and struck senseless. He was anxiously courteous, sending a man to Shepheard's with my written instructions to bring back a change of apparel and offering me every facility for removing my disguise and making myself presentable. The fact that he palpably disbelieved my story did not render his concern one whit the less.

I discovered the hour to be close upon noon, and, once more my outward self, I was about to depart from the Place Bâb el-Khalk, when, into the superintendent's room came Abû Tabâh! His handsome ascetic face exhibited grave concern as he saluted me.

"How can I express my sorrow, Kernaby Pasha," he said in his soft faultless English, "that so unfortunate and unseemly an accident should have befallen you? I learned of your presence here but a few moments ago, and I hastened to convey to you an assurance of my deepest regret and sympathy."

"More than good of you," I replied. "I am much indebted."

"It grieves me," he continued suavely, "to learn that there are footpads infesting the Cairo streets, and that an English gentleman may not walk home from a ball safely. I trust that you will provide the police with a detailed account of any valuables which you may have lost. I have here" — thrusting his hand into his robe — "the only item of your property thus far recovered. No doubt you are somewhat short-sighted, Kernaby Pasha, as I am, and experience a certain difficulty in discerning the names of your partners upon your dance programme."

And with one of those sweet smiles which could so transfigure his face, Abû Tabâh handed me my opera-glasses! ∎

New Kid on the Block

(Continued from page 20)

insisted that I take this one. He didn't need me to find anybody. His strong arms knew more about finding skips as I did. Sammy had just eased me along, waiting to use me for his big kill.

"You looked at me a little too close in Sammy's," I said to the blond guy. "And you followed me too close. It took me till now to figure out why."

I glanced over at Vincent. "I'll take you in. You'll get a much better shake."

"You got the gun with bullets," Vincent said, and he smiled. "But make damn sure you take me to the cops."

"Sammy set you up. Traveler wanted the whole business for himself, right?"

"He wanted my half. Traveler don't even own half anymore. It's in hock to Sammy, and he can't make it up."

I took the thirty-eight from Vincent. I broke it, verified there were no shells, and slipped it into my jacket pocket. He tied the blond guy to the springs of the bed with his shoestrings, and we left the house. I knew he'd break free before the cops came back, but it kept him out of our way for a while.

"You gonna keep his .45?" Vincent said, as we walked the three blocks to the Central Police Station. I had a gun in both pockets and another on my hip.

"Not if he's got a permit," I said.

"Fat chance."

That's what I thought.

The cops took a while but they finally got Traveler and the blond guy in a murder-for-hire scheme. Vincent's wife was Traveler's girl friend and she was two-timing both of them with another of Traveler's creditors.

Chip Vincent was exonerated, but for whatever reason, they couldn't put Sammy in jail. A lot of people knew he was in on it, but there was no proof. All I had was an hunch that the blond guy had come into Sammy's that first morning to get a look at me, but hunches didn't fly in court. Maybe Sammy just paid the right people. He even gave me a bonus for the quick track. I might be wrong about his involvement, but I didn't think so.

I still work the Block now and then, because wayward husbands often make the trip there. I don't work for Sammy anymore though, and he's still slime.   ∎

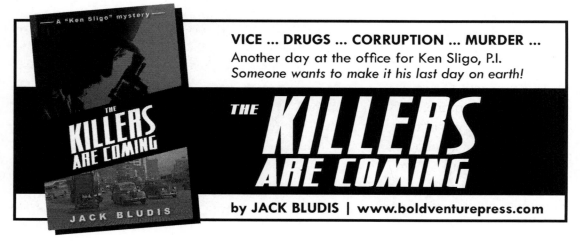

Pursuit of the Moor

(Continued from page 35)

part of a sad ending to his career or his life as Jada feared.

Chapter Three

A Larcenous Lark

"You were supposed to stop him," Jada Hessa all but snarled at me when I returned to my hotel suite after a trip to a cafe for dinner. Once more she was in my room unannounced except by the rush of wind from some open door as I entered. She stepped from the shadows of a corner. "Now you are going to aid him in this madness?"

I was tired from my long walk in the afternoon heat so the allure of this exotic woman was considerably less effective than it had been the night before.

"What else can I do?" I protested. "If I told him not to do it, he would laugh at me. If I told the Caliph's men or the British consulate he would be arrested or worse. My only choice was to go with him to, if I can, to stop him before the fact or help him get out successfully if I cannot."

I could see her stopped by that statement, the emerald fire in her eyes wavering. Her sensual mouth formed a slight smile.

"I was not wrong," she said. "You are a moral man."

I poured myself a drink. "You have too high an opinion of me, Miss Jada-I am not sure I can even get in with him-I saw the seraglio's tower, a young man would have trouble climbing it."

"He will have no trouble in that regard," she smiled slyly. "Not my Roger. It is what

comes after that I fear."

"Me to," I admitted as I gulped my drink and loosened my tie. "I hope I am up to your faith in me." I turned to remove my jacket, but when I turned back, she was gone. I was so tired I did not even look for her.

I met The Moor at the square in the dead of night, dressed, as he had cautioned me, in dark clothes to facilitate the adventure.

"Ready to enter the realm of legend, old fellow?" he asked me. He seemed hail and spry, certainly more ready for the adventure than I.

He had a small satchel over his shoulder but no rope or other of the paraphernalia I had expected from a burglar.

He saw my look and laughed. "What did you expect, old fellow? Grappling hooks and black masks? How droll!"

"Well we are not going to fly up to the tower," I said somewhat edgily.

"Why should we have to?" He asked then held up a key. "I stole it yesterday afternoon. The bleedin' guard thought I was after his wallet but, in fact, I had stolen the key, copied it and was returning it to him. Sleepy fellow on a boring post, don't you know? I let him keep thinking he was safe from theft as he chased me."

He led me across the square to the alley I had first seen him fleeing from. There he halted and looked back to whisper, "Best to be circumspect from this point on, eh, Horatio?"

He flattened against the wall and pointed ahead to the tower, faintly outlined against the starlight.

"There is a door at the base of that wall

beneath the tower," St. Simon whispered. "That is how we enter." He smiled. "I do my homework, old fellow; full plans of the palace memorized."

I followed him with my heart rate rising as we slipped from shadow to shadow until we were flat against the base of the tower wall. He slipped the key into the lock and turned it with a click that sounded like a cannon going off to my over-sensitive ears.

It was pitch dark inside but he grabbed my hand and pulled as we slipped along the narrow, chilled corridor. It was an odd feeling, trusting myself so completely to this old rogue, but he moved though the darkness with the sure-footedness of a cat. I began to wonder if he could see in the dark like one!

After a few moments we came to some sort of panel in the wall. We were suddenly in a very narrow space. It was then that he whispered, "Secret passage, old boy, intended to allow the Caliph to visit his different ladies without the others knowing or going through the main palace."

"How?"

"It was in the blueprints, old fellow," he chuckled.

We moved soft footedly along the narrow space past several peepholes that allowed vision into different of the women's quarters.

Finally, we came to the fifth of the peepholes and stopped. "This is Yasmina's room," my 'host' thief whispered. He worked a simple latch and we entered the boudoir of the 'witch' of the seraglio. Faint starlight was the only illumination in the room, but after the absolute black of the passageway it was a relief.

The room was larger than many whole houses I have seen, strewn with pillows and with a small pool-like-bath in the center of it that extended out onto a wide veranda.

There was no one in sight.

St. Simon put a finger to his lips and pointed toward an alcove where a sleeping woman was reclined on a sumptuous divan. He then indicated a table beside her on which rested a carved wooden box.

The Moor smiled and indicated that I should move to the nightstand to procure the box and I tiptoed across to it. The woman on the bed was on her side, facing away from me and snoring deeply, so I boldly lifted the box. I backed away, my eyes focused on her, almost holding my breath.

When I had backed away from the bed sufficiently, I turned to offer our prize to St. Simon and was shocked to see that he was nowhere to be seen! The Moor had slipped back into the wall panel and was gone!

I was stunned for a moment and unable to think. I looked around, hoping, perhaps, that it was some sort of joke or a misunder-standing, that he would step from the shadows smiling and we would be off for a cocktail at a local cafe.

He did not.

There I stood alone in a strange woman's bedroom with a stolen object in my hands in the palace of an absolute ruler.

I had to get out.

I tried to find the secret passage but there was nothing that indicated where the door might be.

There was a sudden sound on the bed.

I froze.

The woman on the bed rolled over,

snorted, made a grumbling noise, then screamed.

It was the loudest sound I had ever heard!

I gave up looking for the hidden doorway as she continued to yell in Arabic and spun on my heels to head for the doorway into the hall. I stopped short as I heard the thud of booted feet outside the door.

I veered from the doorway and headed out to the veranda at a dead run but skidded to a stop on the slick marble when it was clear there was nowhere to go. I was three stories above a closed courtyard.

By the time I turned around there were three scimitar armed guards, large, muscular women, standing at the arch of the veranda with the now awake woman from the bed.

The 'witch' pointed at me and yelled in Arabic. Even without translation I knew enough to freeze as one of the armed guards ran up, pulled the wooden box from me, then stepped back.

The screaming woman grabbed the box from the guard and immediately opened it to remove the contents. I thought I was going to see the Moorish Mantle but was shocked to see her pull a jeweled tiara from the case.

It had never held the necklace. The thieving Moor had set me up to be caught from the very first!

Chapter Four
Consequence of Crime

I felt like a prized fool as the two burly women guards prodded me along into the heart of the seraglio to, what for all intents and purposes, was an auxiliary throne room.

There, in silken robes was the woman I had come to rob, Yasmina.

She was formidable, to say the least. A raven-haired beauty, older than I expected for the 'favorite wife', in her thirties, but with an hourglass figure beneath the scarlet robe. Her eyes were an odd, swirling gold color and intensely fixed on me as I was brought into the room.

"Why have you invaded our palace?" Yasmina said in perfect English.

"I … uh … " I stammered.

"I came here to see what a seraglio was like on a bet," I lied. "No harm was intended. A silly bet with friends in a pub."

There was a deep silence in the room as the female *ad hoc* ruler considered my absurd statement. It was patently clear it was a lie, but if she was not too vindictive, I had hopes she would accept it to avoid entanglements with the British consulate. I might just escape with my life or my hands intact.

My statement started to be translated by several of the watching women to others who did not understand English. I tried to look as much like a public school stooge as possible, harmless and dilettante, vapid even.

It did not work.

"You are not here to just 'see,' Yasmina said flatly. "You came to steal." She placed a hand on the necklace at her throat that was mostly hidden beneath the collar of her robe. "Perhaps this."

"No … of course not, I … " I began but suddenly the head wife rose to her feet and yelled.

"Do not lie to me!" She waved a hand and the two large female guards stepped in to kick me behind my legs so that I dropped, painfully, into a kneeling position.

"Why did you come here?" She repeated.

I just stared at her, stunned by the viciousness coming from so comely a creature. There was a fiendish light in her eyes that filled me with sudden fear.

"I promise you will tell me everything I want to know," she said. "Take this thieving beast to the stables to contemplate the error of his ways." Yasmina said. "We will summon him when we are more presentable."

I was so stunned that I did not resist when a rope loop was thrown around my neck and I was led from the room down the corridor in a state of shock.

Back stairs led me to the stable below where I was shackled into a small stall that served as a cell.

The guards left me then to stew in my own doubts and let the anger in me rise.

I heard a rush of wind in the corridor outside my stall. It was Jada.

"What did you do?" She asked me accusingly. "You were supposed to stop Roger. Keep him safe."

"Him safe?" I exploded. "Look at me! I'm the one who needs help."

The bight eyed temptress suddenly scowled. "You do not see; Roger did this to draw the vile Yasmina to wear the necklace, she only takes it from her vault for special occasions, when she has to enforce her will. It is the reason she is the Caliph's favorite even though she is not the youngest of his wives."

She moved forward to directly lean her face through the slotted doorway to my stall/ cell. The sensual quality of her features was still there, but there was steel in her voice when she said, "I know Roger did this to force her to take out the necklace and create insecurity in her so she will continue to wear it. That will make it easy for him to seize it. And they will capture him … or worse."

"So, release me," I pleaded. "I can try to find some way to stop him, or at least help him get out."

She seemed about to move to the bar on the outside of the door that latched it closed but stopped and looked up at me. "You must do what you will do on your own … there is a reason … I … I cannot have a direct hand in this."

Suddenly as she had come, she spun on her heels and headed off into the darkness of the stable leaving me alone and angrier still.

And puzzled.

Why couldn't she take a direct hand? Was she so afraid of hurting St. Simon's ego that she would sacrifice me and risk the man's very life?

Chapter Five
Rogue Raid

Abruptly the door to my cell was yanked open and two of the large female guards entered with ropes in hand.

"Come, infidel!" They ordered me. "Our mistress requires your presence for amusement."

Before I realized it, I had a noose over my neck and was being led out of the stall once again to the room where the dark haired Yasmina lounged on her throne-like seat. She had one long, silk trouser encased leg draped over one of the arms of the chair. She was dressed in her regal finest now, her hair done and looking languid.

A younger woman, little more than a girl, was feeding the favorite wife some grapes and gawked as I came into the room. One of the grapes slipped from her fingers and 'missed' her mistress' mouth.

The effect was immediate, Yasmina shot up and slapped the girl hard enough to drive her to her knees. Then, almost as quickly the dark-haired tyrant was back in her seat and looking as languid as she had when I first entered the room.

"Well, infidel beast," Yasmina said. "Have you learned the error of your way and found your tongue? Will you tell the truth now of why you slunk into our quarters or do you wish to amuse us some more?"

There were two other young girls in the room who ran to help the sobbing, kneeling girl up and the two guards who held my 'leash' besides Yasmina.

I noticed that, aside from being 'more together' now, I could clearly see that Yasmina had around her neck the object of my night's actions, The Moorish Mantel!

The object of my nighttime raid was stunning and amazing in person, the three jewels catching and reflecting the light from the room's oil lamps as if they were beacons.

The central stone was a golden-hued diamond flanked by a fiery ruby and an emerald of such brilliance it almost seemed as if they were all illuminated from within.

Why anyone would want to separate the three stones? I wondered. They seemed to be perfectly complementary to each other,

the colors fusing into a tri-hued rainbow when the light hit them correctly.

"Well, infidel?" Yasmina repeated.

I was inclined not to reply but seeing her mercurial reactions, I had no idea what would be worse, confessing now or continuing my silence.

She stared me down and I almost spoke but then the jewels at her neck actually began to pulse with light.

I tried to turn away, tried to resist the flashing lights that seemed to emanate from within the Mantle, but could not. It was if an invisible hand had reached out from within the sparkling crystals to seize me by the throat and pull me forward toward them.

I felt as if I were suddenly seasick and had vertigo at the same time. As the room spun around me, I heard the voice of Yasmina as if from a great distance away.

"You will be the lowest of the low, a beast as befits your status."

Her words came as if from far away, swirling around me like a tornado funnel of sound. They beat against my skin and my eardrums, filled my lungs with a pulsing energy that felt as if it was turning me inside out.

All the eyes of those in the throne room were aghast as the flashing gems continued to cast the tri-rainbow of color at me.

"See, see, the power of the Moorish Mantle," Yasmina said. "And hear my words clearly; you will serve, infidel, as all infidels will. To think I could be trifled with when I have the power of the djinn necklace."

"Djinn necklace?" I muttered before I could stop myself.

She laughed. "I have often summoned

the spirit of the necklace ... the djinn that lives within it ... when I wish to 'correct' wrong behavior. I have barely begun to correct you."

I took this information in, stunned by the developments. Had St. Simon known about the qualities of the necklace when he trapped me into accompanying him?

Once more my eyes were drawn to The Moorish Mantle. I had the fancy that the light was winking at me as if to tell me something.

Perhaps it was my exhaustion or dehydration that made me have that fancy and perhaps they were the reason my eyes wandered from the gem to look past her to one of the interior walls.

The room had heavy hangings on the walls that showed abstract designs, in keeping with Arabic tradition, but my eye was drawn to one that had bright slashes of blue and yellow. The hanging seemed to sway, as if from a breeze, but there was no breeze in the room.

I stared again and again it moved.

There was someone hiding behind the hanging!

I tried not to focus my eyes on that tapestry while trying to determine if it was another menace to me or not.

At the head of the room Yasmina had settled back onto her 'throne' and leered down at me with half lidded eyes. "So, infidel, will you tell me the truth now or shall I show you the true power of my necklace?"

For some reason that made me very angry and, perhaps unwisely I said, "I don't bloody well care what you do or don't show me, ducks."

I had a sudden surge of anger fueled strength and surprised the burly woman to my right with a quick low kick, my shoe hitting her shin hard enough to bring a curse of pain from her and over balance her.

Before the guard to my left could react, I pulled the 'leash' from her hands and struck out at her with a near perfect right hook to her 'manly' jaw. She also fell.

The young servant girls in the room all gasped as one and Yasmina's mouth gaped as I started to run toward her.

One of the servant girls yelled. It seemed to snap the dark haired houri from her shock and she began to speak.

"Necklace, I command ... " she began but just then the tapestry was brushed aside and St. Simon sprang from it yelling at the top of his lungs, "Not at all cricket, Yasmina, to call up the boogyman!"

When the startled first wife tried to reframe her order to the necklace The Moor raised what looked to be an antique blunderbuss! He pulled the trigger and there was a flash of light and smoke.

Yasmina screamed and flew back against the throne-like chair to slump forward, completely still!

My mind was reeling at the developments but I was at a loss as how to react to the man's sudden, violent reappearance.

St. Simon showed no hesitation, however and raced directly to the first wife. It was then I saw that she was not dead, that, in fact, he had not even shot her with a ball, but there was some sort of cloth bag on her stomach.

He saw where my eyes were directed and said, "Not to worry, old fellow; I just gave her a knockout 'blow' to the gut with this bag of rice." He reached around the woman's neck and removed the necklace from the unconscious woman.

The two guards had recovered from their shock and drawn knives but 'The Moor' produced a regular revolver and pointed it at them. "Now, now, ladies … put the cutlery down and turn around … these are not loaded with rice."

The two women had no choice but to comply.

"Let's pop off, shall we, old fellow?" He said then turned on his heels and headed for the balcony of the room.

The servant girls were screaming now, a constant, horrified sound not unlike a siren.

I heard the sound of booted feet pounding down the outer hallway. I had no choice but to follow him.

Out on the balcony he moved quickly to a rope that he had preset and he slipped over the railing. "Hurry, old fellow," he called to me. "Those are the Caliph's guards and they will not be as nice as these ladies were."

"Nice?" I yelled as I dove for the rope.

He ignored my statement and shimmied down the rope with grace that belied his age. I had some difficulty but managed and slid down.

By the time we reached the bottom of the wall the guards above had reached the railing and yelled down at us in Arabic.

St. Simon whirled about and with a deft pull un-hooked his rope so that the guards could not follow us down. "Come on," He ordered and then raced off into the darkness.

We were quickly into the maze-like city around the palace, hidden by shadows in the twisting labyrinthine corridors. We could hear distant pursuit, but just when I worried that they might come close to us, the sneak thief ahead of me pulled me through a doorway and locked the door behind us.

"I am not as young as I once was," the silver haired rogue wheezed as he sat on a wooden bench inside the stable where we had taken refuge. He pulled up a bottle of wine he had previously set there. "This little jaunt wouldn't have even winded me in my heyday."

He took a drink then lit a small lamp. In the flames The Moorish Mantle sparkled with inner life.

"What about me?" I asked. "You almost got me killed."

"You have a heck of a tale to tell, old fellow," he said. "That should satisfy."

"Satisfy?" I yelled, though it came out more as a bray. "You deserted me, abandoned me, sent me on a wild goose chase then threw me to the wolves like a sacrificial lamb."

He gave a roguish chuckle. "That is the worst string of mixed metaphors I've ever heard. Tsk, tsk, and you a journalist!"

His attitude infuriated me. I stomped my boot. "You betrayed me." I reiterated.

"I did no such thing, old fellow," St. Simon said. "I knew that Yasmina kept the necklace in a hidden safe, but I didn't know where. I had to get her to take it out. I could not figure a way to force her to do it, until your selfless act the other day. I knew she would don it to punish a thief."

"But you are the thief!"

"Ah … I think of myself as a recovery agent, it has a better ring." St. Simon said with a jovial smile. "But, as I said, I had to make her get it out. You were just means to accomplish that. I could not have gotten it without you."

He held the necklace up and looked at it intently, moving this way and that to catch the refracted light. "It is the most beautiful thing I have ever seen," he said almost wistfully. "I saw it in that museum and knew I had to hold it. And it has given me my whole career. I … I made the mistake of letting it out of my hands to have it cleaned six years ago and it was taken from me. I was trying to get funds to pursue the thieves when I was captured and spent time in that prison. I thought about this every day I was in there."

He caressed the gems, touched them to his cheek. "I know some will think me mad for it, but I have always felt something more for The Mantle than one would feel for a cold piece of metal. Like … like I had a special connection to it. To others is it is cold but to me … warm as a beating heart. I am afraid I lied to you."

"You bet you did … "

"No … I do not wish to return it to a museum. I … needed to hold this to be sure … but I know now what I must do."

"What?"

"What I incorrectly told you that vixen Yasmina was going to do, but not for the reason she was going to." He produced a jeweler's hammer and chisel.

I couldn't believe what he was going to do; he would destroy The Moorish Mantle!

Epilogue
Crystal Clear

"You can't just whack at a gem like that ruby and get a decent cut. You could shatter it to pieces."

"I know," He said. "I've had five years to study it in my head, to know every flaw and fissure of it. I know exactly what I am doing … I hope."

I couldn't believe he was going to destroy this treasure that had framed his career. I was about to speak about again when I heard a rushing wind sound from out of the shadows of one part of the room.

I turned, expecting to see one of the Caliph's guards coming through a hidden doorway and was stunned to see the fire haired Jada, wrapped in a ruby colored gown that hugged her curvaceous figure, step into the light.

I was once more captured by the presence of the woman, her green eyes almost glowing. She put a finger to her lips when she saw I was going to speak and then pointed to St. Simon who was bent over the necklace, intent on his work.

He raised the hammer and inhaled.

I held my breath.

Jada stood, her eyes fixed on the necklace as if her life depended on it.

The hammer fell and struck the chisel.

It seemed to me as if the world went silent at that moment, as if time slowed and every part of my consciousness was drawn to the edge of the chisel where it met the ruby.

There was a cracking sound and Jada gasped, grabbing her stomach and stumbled forward.

"Roger!" She called in a breathless and pain wracked voice.

St. Simon shot up from his seat and starred at her as if he had never seen her before, then ran to her side.

"You are real." He spoke in a voice that sounded curiously like a child's. He grabbed her shoulders and helped her straighten up.

Her face was radiant, her smile glowing and her eyes emerald beacons.

"Yes, Roger," she said. "I am real. And thanks to you I am now free."

"What is going on?" I asked.

The two stared into each other's eyes as if they had never seen each other before, as if the world could come to a stop and they would not care.

After a long moment St. Simon said, "All the years of my career they all said I had some special luck, a guardian angel. I was never caught, life went well for me, it was all a thrill, fun. Always there was an image in my mind, a ghost woman, my dream girl, I guess you'd say. I would talk to her, dream a future with her. And, sometimes I would imagine I heard her." He ran a hand along Jada's jawline as if he was afraid she would disappear and wanted to memorize it.

"It was not until I lost the necklace and I was locked away that I heard that voice clearly."

"My voice," Jada said. "Since he first stole the necklace that was my prison and my home I knew that I had a special connection with Roger. After all the centuries trapped in the necklace, slave to any who possessed it and knew how to summon its

power I knew this connection was more.

"He did not know how to summon the power of the necklace, but I could 'help him' in little ways. And I did. When he foolishly let the necklace leave his hands, I knew what you mortals feel with the loss of hope. I reached out to his mind and told him what he must do to free me."

"So, you see, Horatio, old fellow," St. Simon said. "Why I had to get the necklace; to see if the voice in my head was real or I had simply been driven mad in that jail."

He never took his eyes off her. "And I am mad, but not like I thought. To have had this immortal angel in my grasp and yet unseen all these years."

"No angel," Jada said. "But a Djinn and immortal no more." She walked with St. Simon toward the door of the stable. A gush of wind blew her flaming hair aside to reveal a delicate ear that came to a point.

She saw me look and said, "As with Solomon's wife we of fire and flame cannot assume a perfect human form."

"It is perfect for me," the old rogue said.

She held St. Simon's hand to her cheek. "I shall live as one of you and grow old and die with my Roger."

"And I with you," he said. He looked back at me and smiled once more that roguish smile. "And so you have a heck of a tale to tell, eh, old fellow?"

Indeed, I have. And now you have read it. As to where the two have gone … I do not know and if I did I would not tell, but where ever it is, I know they are happy, as I hope someday I shall be, in the arms of a perfect love like theirs. ∎

Captain Warwick's Hand

(Continued from page 74)

He paused for a moment in thought before going on. "What would such treasure mean for an under-fed, castrated slave? In the village the lot of you came from, I assure you, it is enough for a roof and bread for the rest of your life. It was more than such a man would ever see … at the expense of his own hand."

Palgrave spoke. "So you were given the hand of a eunuch."

"Nay, mate. The sultan called for volunteers. But they had no tongues to speak — the sultan had them cut out when they were children — and no desire arose on the face of any."

Water trickling from the roof slowed to a steady drip, splashing into a puddle on the dirt floor.

"One voice broke the silence. A concubine stood and stepped forward. 'I accept the offer, my Pasha.'"

"A woman?" I asked.

Warwick nodded. "'Very well, Guzel,' he said. 'Take the pearls in exchange for your hand. I banish you from Arabia.'"

He took the glove off again. The hand looked even smaller and more delicate now.

"Have you ever watched a hand severed from the limb? Monstrous violence. The guard needed several blows from his scimitar, and they sawed at it, pulled, and twisted, until it finally broke free of the bone. The blood — there was so much blood — and her screams still echo in my memory."

The noise of rain softened to silence.

The slow drip stopped.

"Fingers moved even after the hand was cut free. It resembled nothing so much as a five-legged spider or a crab cut from its claws."

"What happened to Guzel?" I asked.

"The harem girl? She would have known that the sultan would not keep her — allowing the freedom she longed for — but she did not plan out a new life. Fearing the sultan would become jealous, men of Tascara did not speak to her. The women refused, too, as she had chosen to be deformed rather than stay in the company of the sultan. She was all alone."

Palgave began, "But the pearls — "

"The pearls could not provide her comfort. And having never purchased anything before, she was quickly swindled out of several, and outright robbed of even more. Each pearl she lost was a painfully paid expense of freedom."

I wondered, was it so bad to be among the harem? To never worry about food, drink, or shelter?

"I felt pity and took her aboard when she had no pearls left and I was ready to sail. But she was too beautiful to safely keep aboard the *Shadow* with its rough men. She had to return to land, yet was helpless without knowledge beyond the sultan's palace. Last I recollect, she joined a brothel in Tangier."

Daylight glowed through the holes in the roof like a constellation in the night sky.

He added, "Everything has a price, even your life. Be careful how you choose to spend it." ■

Tunnel Under the World
(Continued from page 66)

apprehensive and soothing. She kissed him good-by as he hurried out to the bus without another word.

Miss Mitkin, at the reception desk, greeted him with a yawn. "Morning," she said drowsily. "Mr. Barth won't be in today."

Burckhardt started to say something, but checked himself. She would not know that Barth hadn't been in yesterday, either, because she was tearing a June 14th pad off her calendar to make way for the "new" June 15th sheet.

He staggered to his own desk and stared unseeingly at the morning's mail. It had not even been opened yet, but he knew that the Factory Distributors envelope contained an order for twenty thousand feet of the new acoustic tile, and the one from Finebeck & Sons was a complaint.

After a long while, he forced himself to open them. They were.

By lunchtime, driven by a desperate sense of urgency, Burckhardt made Miss Mitkin take her lunch hour first—the June-fifteenth-that-was-yesterday, *he* had gone first. She went, looking vaguely worried about his strained insistence, but it made no difference to Burckhardt's mood.

The phone rang and Burckhardt picked it up abstractedly. "Contro Chemicals Downtown, Burckhardt speaking."

The voice said, "This is Swanson," and stopped.

Burckhardt waited expectantly, but that was all. He said, "Hello?"

Again the pause. Then Swanson asked

in sad resignation, "Still nothing, eh?"

"Nothing what? Swanson, is there something you want? You came up to me yesterday and went through this routine. You—"

The voice crackled: "Burckhardt! Oh, my good heavens, *you remember*! Stay right there—I'll be down in half an hour!"

"What's this all about?"

"Never mind," the little man said exultantly. "Tell you about it when I see you. Don't say any more over the phone—somebody may be listening. Just wait there. Say, hold on a minute. Will you be alone in the office?"

"Well, no. Miss Mitkin will probably—"

"Hell. Look, Burckhardt, where do you eat lunch? Is it good and noisy?"

"Why, I suppose so. The Crystal Cafe. It's just about a block—"

"I know where it is. Meet you in half an hour!" And the receiver clicked.

The Crystal Cafe was no longer painted red, but the temperature was still up. And they had added piped-in music interspersed with commercials. The advertisements were for Frosty-Flip, Marlin Cigarettes—"They're sanitized," the announcer purred—and something called Choco-Bite candy bars that Burckhardt couldn't remember ever having heard of before. But he heard more about them quickly enough.

While he was waiting for Swanson to show up, a girl in the cellophane skirt of a nightclub cigarette vendor came through the restaurant with a tray of tiny scarlet-wrapped candies.

"Choco-Bites are *tangy*," she was murmuring as she came close to his table. "Choco-Bites are *tangier* than tangy!"

Burckhardt, intent on watching for the strange little man who had phoned him, paid little attention. But as she scattered a handful of the confections over the table next to his, smiling at the occupants, he caught a glimpse of her and turned to stare.

"Why, Miss Horn!" he said.

The girl dropped her tray of candies.

Burckhardt rose, concerned over the girl. "Is something wrong?"

But she fled.

The manager of the restaurant was staring suspiciously at Burckhardt, who sank back in his seat and tried to look inconspicuous. He hadn't insulted the girl! Maybe she was just a very strictly reared young lady, he thought—in spite of the long bare legs under the cellophane skirt—and when he addressed her, she thought he was a masher.

Ridiculous idea. Burckhardt scowled uneasily and picked up his menu.

"Burckhardt!" It was a shrill whisper.

Burckhardt looked up over the top of his menu, startled. In the seat across from him, the little man named Swanson was sitting, tensely poised.

"Burckhardt!" the little man whispered again. "Let's get out of here! They're on to you now. If you want to stay alive, come on!"

There was no arguing with the man. Burckhardt gave the hovering manager a sick, apologetic smile and followed Swanson out. The little man seemed to know where he was going. In the street, he clutched Burckhardt by the elbow and hurried him off down the block.

"Did you see her?" he demanded. "That Horn woman, in the phone booth? She'll have them here in five minutes, believe me, so hurry it up!"

Although the street was full of people and cars, nobody was paying any attention to Burckhardt and Swanson. The air had a nip in it—more like October than June, Burckhardt thought, in spite of the weather bureau. And he felt like a fool, following this mad little man down the street, running away from some "them" toward—toward what? The little man might be crazy, but he was afraid. And the fear was infectious.

"In here!" panted the little man.

It was another restaurant—more of a bar, really, and a sort of second-rate place that Burckhardt had never patronized.

"Right straight through," Swanson whispered; and Burckhardt, like a biddable boy, side-stepped through the mass of tables to the far end of the restaurant.

It was "L"-shaped, with a front on two streets at right angles to each other. They came out on the side street, Swanson staring coldly back at the question-looking cashier, and crossed to the opposite sidewalk.

They were under the marquee of a movie theater. Swanson's expression began to relax.

"Lost them!" he crowed softly. "We're almost there."

He stepped up to the window and bought two tickets. Burckhardt trailed him in to the theater. It was a weekday matinee and the place was almost empty. From the screen came sounds of gunfire and horse's hoofs. A solitary usher, leaning against a bright brass rail, looked briefly at them and went back to staring boredly at the picture as Swanson led Burckhardt down a flight of carpeted marble steps.

They were in the lounge and it was empty. There was a door for men and one for ladies; and there was a third door, marked "MANAGER" in gold letters. Swanson listened at the door, and gently opened it and peered inside.

"Okay," he said, gesturing.

Burckhardt followed him through an empty office, to another door—a closet, probably, because it was unmarked.

But it was no closet. Swanson opened it warily, looked inside, then motioned Burckhardt to follow.

It was a tunnel, metal-walled, brightly lit. Empty, it stretched vacantly away in both directions from them.

Burckhardt looked wondering around. One thing he knew and knew full well:

No such tunnel belonged under Tylerton.

There was a room off the tunnel with chairs and a desk and what looked like television screens. Swanson slumped in a chair, panting.

"We're all right for a while here," he wheezed. "They don't come here much any more. If they do, we'll hear them and we can hide."

"Who?" demanded Burckhardt.

The little man said, "Martians!" His voice cracked on the word and the life seemed to go out of him. In morose tones, he went on: "Well, I think they're Martians. Although you could be right, you know; I've had plenty of time to think it over these last few weeks, after they got you, and it's possible they're Russians after all. Still—"

"Start from the beginning. Who got me when?"

Swanson sighed. "So we have to go through the whole thing again. All right. It was about two months ago that you banged on my door, late at night. You were all beat up—scared silly. You begged me to help you—"

"*I* did?"

"Naturally you don't remember any of this. Listen and you'll understand. You were talking a blue streak about being captured and threatened, and your wife being dead and coming back to life, and all kinds of mixed-up nonsense. I thought you were crazy. But—well, I've always had a lot of respect for you. And you begged me to hide you and I have this darkroom, you know. It locks from the inside only. I put the lock on myself. So we went in there—just to humor you—and along about midnight, which was only fifteen or twenty minutes after, we passed out."

"Passed out?"

Swanson nodded. "Both of us. It was like being hit with a sandbag. Look, didn't that happen to you again last night?"

"I guess it did," Burckhardt shook his head uncertainly.

"Sure. And then all of a sudden we were awake again, and you said you were going to show me something funny, and we went out and bought a paper. And the date on it was June 15th."

"June 15th? But that's today! I mean—"

"You got it, friend. It's always today!"

It took time to penetrate.

Burckhardt said wonderingly, "You've hidden out in that darkroom for how many weeks?"

"How can I tell? Four or five, maybe. I lost count. And every day the same—always the 15th of June, always my land-lady, Mrs. Keefer, is sweeping the front steps, always the same headline in the papers at the corner. It gets monotonous, friend."

IV

It was Burckhardt's idea and Swanson despised it, but he went along. He was the type who always went along.

"It's dangerous," he grumbled worriedly. "Suppose somebody comes by? They'll spot us and—"

"What have we got to lose?"

Swanson shrugged. "It's dangerous," he said again. But he went along.

Burckhardt's idea was very simple. He was sure of only one thing—the tunnel went somewhere. Martians or Russians, fantastic plot or crazy hallucination, whatever was wrong with Tylerton had an explanation, and the place to look for it was at the end of the tunnel.

They jogged along. It was more than a mile before they began to see an end. They were in luck—at least no one came through the tunnel to spot them. But Swanson had said that it was only at certain hours that the tunnel seemed to be in use.

Always the fifteenth of June. Why? Burckhardt asked himself. Never mind the how. *Why?*

And falling asleep, completely invol-untarily—everyone at the same time, it seemed. And not remembering, never remembering anything—Swanson had said how eagerly he saw Burckhardt again, the morning after Burckhardt had incautiously waited five minutes too many before retreating into the darkroom. When Swanson had come to, Burckhardt was gone. Swanson had seen him in the street that afternoon, but Burckhardt had remem-bered nothing.

And Swanson had lived his mouse's existence for weeks, hiding in the wood-work at night, stealing out by day to search for Burckhardt in pitiful hope, scurrying around the fringe of life, trying to keep from the deadly eyes of *them*.

Them. One of "them" was the girl named April Horn. It was by seeing her walk carelessly into a telephone booth and never come out that Swanson had found the tunnel. Another was the man at the cigar stand in Burckhardt's office building. There were more, at least a dozen that Swanson knew of or suspected.

They were easy enough to spot, once you knew where to look—for they, alone in Tylerton, changed their roles from day to day. Burckhardt was on that 8:51 bus, every morning of every day-that-was-June-15th, never different by a hair or a moment. But April Horn was sometimes gaudy in the cellophane skirt, giving away candy or cigarettes; sometimes plainly dressed; sometimes not seen by Swanson at all.

Russians? Martians? Whatever they were, what could they be hoping to gain from this mad masquerade?

Burckhardt didn't know the answer—but perhaps it lay beyond the door at the end of the tunnel. They listened carefully and heard distant sounds that could not quite be made out, but nothing that seemed dangerous. They slipped through.

And, through a wide chamber and up a flight of steps, they found they were in what Burckhardt recognized as the Contro Chemicals plant.

Nobody was in sight. By itself, that was not so very odd—the automatized factory had never had very many persons in it. But Burckhardt remembered, from his single visit, the endless, ceaseless busyness of the plant, the valves that opened and closed, the vats that emptied themselves and filled themselves and stirred and cooked and chemically tasted the bubbling liquids they held inside themselves. The plant was never populated, but it was never still.

Only—now it *was* still. Except for the distant sounds, there was no breath of life in it. The captive electronic minds were sending out no commands; the coils and relays were at rest.

Burckhardt said, "Come on." Swanson reluctantly followed him through the tangled aisles of stainless-steel columns and tanks.

They walked as though they were in the presence of the dead. In a way, they were, for what were the automatons that once had run the factory, if not corpses? The machines were controlled by computers that were really not computers at all, but the electronic analogues of living brains. And if they were turned off, were they not dead? For each had once been a human mind.

Take a master petroleum chemist, infinitely skilled in the separation of crude oil into its fractions. Strap him down, probe into his brain with searching electronic needles. The machine scans the patterns of the mind, translates what it sees into charts and sine waves. Impress these same waves on a robot computer and you have your chemist. Or a thousand copies of your chemist, if you wish, with all of his knowledge and skill, and no human limitations at all.

Put a dozen copies of him into a plant and they will run it all, twenty-four hours a day, seven days of every week, never tiring, never overlooking anything, never forgetting....

Swanson stepped up closer to Burckhardt. "I'm scared," he said.

They were across the room now and the sounds were louder. They were not machine sounds, but voices; Burckhardt moved cautiously up to a door and dared to peer around it.

It was a smaller room, lined with television screens, each one—a dozen or more, at least—with a man or woman sitting before it, staring into the screen and dictating notes into a recorder. The viewers dialed from scene to scene; no two screens ever showed the same picture.

The pictures seemed to have little in common. One was a store, where a girl dressed like April Horn was demonstrating home freezers. One was a series of shots of kitchens. Burckhardt caught a glimpse of what looked like the cigar stand in his office building.

It was baffling and Burckhardt would have loved to stand there and puzzle it out, but it was too busy a place. There was the chance that someone would look their way or walk out and find them.

They found another room. This one was empty. It was an office, large and sumptuous. It had a desk, littered with papers. Burckhardt stared at them, briefly at first—then, as the words on one of them caught his attention, with incredulous fascination.

He snatched up the topmost sheet, scanned it, and another, while Swanson was frenziedly searching through the drawers.

Burckhardt swore unbelievingly and dropped the papers to the desk.

Swanson, hardly noticing, yelped with delight: "Look!" He dragged a gun from the desk. "And it's loaded, too!"

Burckhardt stared at him blankly, trying to assimilate what he had read. Then, as he realized what Swanson had said, Burckhardt's eyes sparked. "Good man!" he cried. "We'll take it. We're getting out of here with that gun, Swanson. And we're going to the police! Not the cops in Tylerton, but the F.B.I., maybe. Take a look at this!"

The sheaf he handed Swanson was headed: "Test Area Progress Report. Subject: Marlin Cigarettes Campaign." It was mostly tabulated figures that made little sense to Burckhardt and Swanson, but at the end was a summary that said:

Although Test 47-K3 pulled nearly double the number of new users of any of the other tests conducted, it probably cannot be used in the field because of local sound-truck control ordinances.

The tests in the 47-K12 group were second best and our recommendation is that retests be conducted in this appeal, testing each of the three best campaigns with and without the addition of sampling techniques.

An alternative suggestion might be to proceed directly with the top appeal in the K12 series, if the client is unwilling to go to the expense of additional tests.

All of these forecast expectations have an 80% probability of being within one-half of one per cent of results forecast, and more than 99% probability of coming within 5%.

Swanson looked up from the paper into Burckhardt's eyes. "I don't get it," he complained.

Burckhardt said, "I don't blame you. It's crazy, but it fits the facts, Swanson, *it fits the facts*. They aren't Russians and they aren't Martians. These people are advertising men! Somehow—heaven knows how they did it—they've taken Tylerton over. They've got us, all of us, you and me and twenty or thirty thousand other people, right under their thumbs.

"Maybe they hypnotize us and maybe it's something else; but however they do it, what happens is that they let us live a day at a time. They pour advertising into us the whole damned day long. And at the end of the day, they see what happened—and then they wash the day out of our minds and start again the next day with different advertising."

Swanson's jaw was hanging. He managed to close it and swallow. "Nuts!" he said flatly.

Burckhardt shook his head. "Sure, it sounds crazy—but this whole thing is crazy. How else would you explain it? You can't deny that most of Tylerton lives the same day over and over again. You've *seen* it! And that's the crazy part and we have to admit that that's true—unless we are the crazy ones. And once you admit that somebody, somehow, knows how to accomplish that, the rest of it makes all kinds of sense.

"Think of it, Swanson! They test every last detail before they spend a nickel on advertising! Do you have any idea what that means? Lord knows how much money is involved, but I know for a fact that some companies spend twenty or thirty million dollars a year on advertising. Multiply it, say, by a hundred companies. Say that every one of them learns how to cut its advertising cost by only ten per cent. And that's peanuts, believe me!

"If they know in advance what's going to work, they can cut their costs in half—maybe to less than half, I don't know. But that's saving two or three hundred million dollars a year—and if they pay only ten or twenty per cent of that for the use of Tylerton, it's still dirt cheap for them and a fortune for whoever took over Tylerton."

Swanson licked his lips. "You mean," he offered hesitantly, "that we're a—well, a kind of captive audience?"

Burckhardt frowned. "Not exactly." He thought for a minute. "You know how a doctor tests something like penicillin? He sets up a series of little colonies of germs on gelatine disks and he tries the stuff on one after another, changing it a little each time. Well, that's us—we're the germs, Swanson. Only it's even more efficient than that. They don't have to test more than one colony, because they can use it over and over again."

It was too hard for Swanson to take in. He only said: "What do we do about it?"

"We go to the police. They can't use human beings for guinea pigs!"

"How do we get to the police?"

Burckhardt hesitated. "I think—" he began slowly. "Sure. This place is the office of somebody important. We've got a gun. We'll stay right here until he comes along. And he'll get us out of here."

Simple and direct. Swanson subsided and found a place to sit, against the wall, out of sight of the door. Burckhardt took up a position behind the door itself—

And waited.

The wait was not as long as it might have been. Half an hour, perhaps. Then Burckhardt heard approaching voices and had time for a swift whisper to Swanson before he flattened himself against the wall.

It was a man's voice, and a girl's. The man was saying, "—reason why you couldn't report on the phone? You're ruining your whole day's test! What the devil's the matter with you, Janet?"

"I'm sorry, Mr. Dorchin," she said in a sweet, clear tone. "I thought it was important."

The man grumbled, "Important! One lousy unit out of twenty-one thousand."

"But it's the Burckhardt one, Mr. Dorchin. Again. And the way he got out of sight, he must have had some help."

"All right, all right. It doesn't matter, Janet; the Choco-Bite program is ahead of schedule anyhow. As long as you're this far, come on in the office and make out your worksheet. And don't worry about the Burckhardt business. He's probably just wandering around. We'll pick him up tonight and—"

They were inside the door. Burckhardt kicked it shut and pointed the gun.

"That's what you think," he said triumphantly.

It was worth the terrified hours, the bewildered sense of insanity, the confusion and fear. It was the most satisfying sensation Burckhardt had ever had in his life. The expression on the man's face was one he had read about but never actually seen: Dorchin's mouth fell open and his eyes went wide, and though he managed to make a sound that might have been a question, it was not in words.

The girl was almost as surprised. And Burckhardt, looking at her, knew why her voice had been so familiar. The girl was the one who had introduced herself to him as April Horn.

Dorchin recovered himself quickly. "Is this the one?" he asked sharply.

The girl said, "Yes."

Dorchin nodded. "I take it back. You were right. Uh, you—Burckhardt. What do you want?"

Swanson piped up, "Watch him! He might have another gun."

"Search him then," Burckhardt said. "I'll tell you what we want, Dorchin. We want you to come along with us to the FBI and explain to them how you can get away with kidnapping twenty thousand people."

"Kidnapping?" Dorchin snorted. "That's ridiculous, man! Put that gun away—you can't get away with this!"

Burckhardt hefted the gun grimly. "I think I can."

Dorchin looked furious and sick—but, oddly, not afraid. "Damn it—" he started to bellow, then closed his mouth and swallowed. "Listen," he said persuasively, "you're making a big mistake. I haven't kidnapped anybody, believe me!"

"I don't believe you," said Burckhardt bluntly. "Why should I?"

"But it's true! Take my word for it!"

Burckhardt shook his head. "The FBI can take your word if they like. We'll find out. Now how do we get out of here?"

Dorchin opened his mouth to argue.

Burckhardt blazed: "Don't get in my way! I'm willing to kill you if I have to. Don't you understand that? I've gone through two days of hell and every second of it I blame on you. Kill you? It would be a pleasure and I don't have a thing in the world to lose! Get us out of here!"

Dorchin's face went suddenly opaque. He seemed about to move; but the blonde girl he had called Janet slipped between him and the gun.

"Please!" she begged Burckhardt. "You don't understand. You mustn't shoot!"

"*Get out of my way!*"

"But, Mr. Burckhardt—"

She never finished. Dorchin, his face unreadable, headed for the door. Burckhardt had been pushed one degree too far. He swung the gun, bellowing. The girl called out sharply. He pulled the trigger. Closing on him with pity and pleading in her eyes, she came again between the gun and the man.

Burckhardt aimed low instinctively, to cripple, not to kill. But his aim was not good.

The pistol bullet caught her in the pit of the stomach.

Dorchin was out and away, the door slamming behind him, his footsteps racing into the distance.

Burckhardt hurled the gun across the room and jumped to the girl.

Swanson was moaning. "That finishes us, Burckhardt. Oh, why did you do it? We could have got away. We could have gone to the police. We were practically out of here! We—"

Burckhardt wasn't listening. He was kneeling beside the girl. She lay flat on her back, arms helter-skelter. There was no blood, hardly any sign of the wound; but the position in which she lay was one that

no living human being could have held.

Yet she wasn't dead.

She wasn't dead—and Burckhardt, frozen beside her, thought: *She isn't alive, either.*

There was no pulse, but there was a rhythmic ticking of the outstretched fingers of one hand.

There was no sound of breathing, but there was a hissing, sizzling noise.

The eyes were open and they were looking at Burckhardt. There was neither fear nor pain in them, only a pity deeper than the Pit.

She said, through lips that writhed erratically, "Don't—worry, Mr. Burckhardt. I'm—all right."

Burckhardt rocked back on his haunches, staring. Where there should have been blood, there was a clean break of a substance that was not flesh; and a curl of thin golden-copper wire.

Burckhardt moistened his lips.

"You're a robot," he said.

The girl tried to nod. The twitching lips said, "I am. And so are you."

V

Swanson, after a single inarticulate sound, walked over to the desk and sat staring at the wall. Burckhardt rocked back and forth beside the shattered puppet on the floor. He had no words.

The girl managed to say, "I'm—sorry all this happened." The lovely lips twisted into a rictus sneer, frightening on that smooth young face, until she got them under control. "Sorry," she said again. "The—nerve center was right about where the bullet hit. Makes it difficult to—control this body."

Burckhardt nodded automatically, accepting the apology. Robots. It was obvious, now that he knew it. In hindsight, it was inevitable. He thought of his mystic notions of hypnosis or Martians or something stranger still—idiotic, for the simple fact of created robots fitted the facts better and more economically.

All the evidence had been before him. The automatized factory, with its transplanted minds—why not transplant a mind into a humanoid robot, give it its original owner's features and form?

Could it know that it was a robot?

"All of us," Burckhardt said, hardly aware that he spoke out loud. "My wife and my secretary and you and the neighbors. All of us the same."

"No." The voice was stronger. "Not exactly the same, all of us. I chose it, you see. I—" this time the convulsed lips were not a random contortion of the nerves—"I was an ugly woman, Mr. Burckhardt, and nearly sixty years old. Life had passed me. And when Mr. Dorchin offered me the chance to live again as a beautiful girl, I jumped at the opportunity. Believe me, I *jumped*, in spite of its disadvantages. My flesh body is still alive—it is sleeping, while I am here. I could go back to it. But I never do."

"And the rest of us?"

"Different, Mr. Burckhardt. I work here. I'm carrying out Mr. Dorchin's orders, mapping the results of the advertising tests, watching you and the others live as he makes you live. I do it by choice, but you have no choice. Because, you see, you are dead."

"Dead?" cried Burckhardt; it was almost a scream.

The blue eyes looked at him unwinkingly and he knew that it was no lie. He swallowed, marveling at the intricate mechanisms that let him swallow, and sweat, and eat.

He said: "Oh. The explosion in my dream."

"It was no dream. You are right—the explosion. That was real and this plant was the cause of it. The storage tanks let go and what the blast didn't get, the fumes killed a little later. But almost everyone died in the blast, twenty-one thousand persons. You died with them and that was Dorchin's chance."

"The damned ghoul!" said Burckhardt.

The twisted shoulders shrugged with an odd grace. "Why? You were gone. And you and all the others were what Dorchin wanted—a whole town, a perfect slice of America. It's as easy to transfer a pattern from a dead brain as a living one. Easier—the dead can't say no. Oh, it took work and money—the town was a wreck—but it was possible to rebuild it entirely, especially because it wasn't necessary to have all the details exact.

"There were the homes where even the brains had been utterly destroyed, and those are empty inside, and the cellars that needn't be too perfect, and the streets that hardly matter. And anyway, it only has to last for one day. The same day—June 15th—over and over again; and if someone finds something a little wrong, somehow, the discovery won't have time to snowball, wreck the validity of the tests, because all errors are canceled out at midnight."

The face tried to smile. "That's the dream, Mr. Burckhardt, that day of June 15th, because you never really lived it. It's a present from Mr. Dorchin, a dream that he gives you and then takes back at the end of the day, when he has all his figures on how many of you responded to what variation of which appeal, and the maintenance crews go down the tunnel to go through the whole city, washing out the new dream with their little electronic drains, and then the dream starts all over again. On June 15th.

"Always June 15th, because June 14th is the last day any of you can remember alive. Sometimes the crews miss someone—as they missed you, because you were under your boat. But it doesn't matter. The ones who are missed give themselves away if they show it—and if they don't, it doesn't affect the test. But they don't drain us, the ones of us who work for Dorchin. We sleep when the power is turned off, just as you do. When we wake up, though, we remember." The face contorted wildly. "If I could only forget!"

Burckhardt said unbelievingly, "All this to sell merchandise! It must have cost millions!"

The robot called April Horn said, "It did. But it has made millions for Dorchin, too. And that's not the end of it. Once he finds the master words that make people act, do you suppose he will stop with that? Do you suppose—"

The door opened, interrupting her. Burckhardt whirled. Belatedly remembering Dorchin's flight, he raised the gun.

"Don't shoot," ordered the voice calmly. It was not Dorchin; it was another robot, this one not disguised with the clever plastics and cosmetics, but shining plain. It said metallically: "Forget it, Burckhardt. You're not accomplishing anything. Give me that gun before you do any more damage. Give it to me *now*."

Burckhardt bellowed angrily. The gleam on this robot torso was steel; Burckhardt was not at all sure that his bullets would pierce it, or do much harm if they did. He would have put it to the test—

But from behind him came a whimpering, scurrying whirlwind; its name was Swanson, hysterical with fear. He catapulted into Burckhardt and sent him sprawling, the gun flying free.

"Please!" begged Swanson incoherently, prostrate before the steel robot. "He would have shot you—please don't hurt me! Let me work for you, like that girl. I'll do anything, anything you tell me—"

The robot voice said. "We don't need your help." It took two precise steps and stood over the gun—and spurned it, left it lying on the floor.

The wrecked blonde robot said, without emotion, "I doubt that I can hold out much longer, Mr. Dorchin."

"Disconnect if you have to," replied the steel robot.

Burckhardt blinked. "But you're not Dorchin!"

The steel robot turned deep eyes on him. "I am," it said. "Not in the flesh—but this is the body I am using at the moment. I doubt that you can damage this one with the gun. The other robot body was more vulnerable. Now will you stop this nonsense? I don't want to have to damage you; you're too expensive for that. Will you just sit down and let the maintenance crews adjust you?"

Swanson groveled. "You—you won't punish us?"

The steel robot had no expression, but its voice was almost surprised. "Punish you?" it repeated on a rising note. "How?"

Swanson quivered as though the word had been a whip; but Burckhardt flared: "Adjust *him*, if he'll let you—but not me! You're going to have to do me a lot of damage, Dorchin. I don't care what I cost or how much trouble it's going to be to put me back together again. But I'm going out of that door! If you want to stop me, you'll have to kill me. You won't stop me any other way!"

The steel robot took a half-step toward him, and Burckhardt involuntarily checked his stride. He stood poised and shaking, ready for death, ready for attack, ready for anything that might happen.

Ready for anything except what did happen. For Dorchin's steel body merely stepped aside, between Burckhardt and the gun, but leaving the door free.

"Go ahead," invited the steel robot. "Nobody's stopping you."

Outside the door, Burckhardt brought up sharp. It was insane of Dorchin to let him go! Robot or flesh, victim or beneficiary, there was nothing to stop him from going to the FBI or whatever law he could find away from Dorchin's synthetic empire, and telling his story. Surely the corporations who paid Dorchin for test results had no notion of the ghoul's technique he used; Dorchin would have to keep it from them, for the breath of publicity would put a stop to it. Walking out meant death, perhaps—but at that moment in his pseudo-life, death was no terror for Burckhardt.

There was no one in the corridor. He found a window and stared out of it. There was Tylerton—an ersatz city, but looking so real and familiar that Burckhardt almost imagined the whole episode a dream. It was no dream, though. He was certain of that in his heart and equally certain that nothing in Tylerton could help him now.

It had to be the other direction.

It took him a quarter of an hour to find a way, but he found it—skulking through the corridors, dodging the suspicion of footsteps, knowing for certain that his hiding was in vain, for Dorchin was undoubtedly aware of every move he made. But no one stopped him, and he found another door.

It was a simple enough door from the inside. But when he opened it and stepped out, it was like nothing he had ever seen.

First there was light—brilliant, incredible, blinding light. Burckhardt blinked upward, unbelieving and afraid.

He was standing on a ledge of smooth, finished metal. Not a dozen yards from his feet, the ledge dropped sharply away; he hardly dared approach the brink, but even from where he stood he could see no bottom to the chasm before him. And the gulf extended out of sight into the glare on either side of him.

No wonder Dorchin could so easily give him his freedom! From the factory, there was nowhere to go—but how incredible this fantastic gulf, how impossible the hundred white and blinding suns that hung above!

A voice by his side said inquiringly, "Burckhardt?" And thunder rolled the name, mutteringly soft, back and forth in the abyss before him.

Burckhardt wet his lips. "Y-yes?" he croaked.

"This is Dorchin. Not a robot this time, but Dorchin in the flesh, talking to you on a hand mike. Now you have seen, Burckhardt. Now will you be reasonable and let the maintenance crews take over?"

Burckhardt stood paralyzed. One of the moving mountains in the blinding glare came toward him.

It towered hundreds of feet over his head; he stared up at its top, squinting helplessly into the light.

It looked like—

Impossible!

The voice in the loudspeaker at the door said, "Burckhardt?" But he was unable to answer.

A heavy rumbling sigh. "I see," said the voice. "You finally understand. There's no place to go. You know it now. I could have told you, but you might not have believed me, so it was better for you to see it yourself. And after all, Burckhardt, why would I reconstruct a city just the way it was before? I'm a businessman; I count costs. If a thing has to be full-scale, I build it that way. But there wasn't any need to in this case."

From the mountain before him, Burckhardt helplessly saw a lesser cliff descend carefully toward him. It was long and dark, and at the end of it was whiteness, five-fingered whiteness....

"Poor little Burckhardt," crooned the loudspeaker, while the echoes rumbled through the enormous chasm that was only a workshop. "It must have been quite a shock for you to find out you were living in a town built on a table top."

VI

It was the morning of June 15th, and Guy Burckhardt woke up screaming out of a dream.

It had been a monstrous and incomprehensible dream, of explosions and shadowy figures that were not men and terror beyond words.

He shuddered and opened his eyes.

Outside his bedroom window, a hugely amplified voice was howling.

Burckhardt stumbled over to the window and stared outside. There was an out-of-season chill to the air, more like October than June; but the scent was normal enough — except for the sound-truck that squatted at curbside halfway down the block. Its speaker horns blared:

"Are you a coward? Are you a fool? Are you going to let crooked politicians steal the country from you? NO! Are you going to put up with four more years of graft and crime? NO! Are you going to vote straight Federal Party all up and down the ballot? YES! *You just bet you are!*"

Sometimes he screams, sometimes he wheedles, threatens, begs, cajoles ... but his voice goes on and on through one June 15th after another. ∎

An Old Friend
(Continued from page 26)

onslaught was about to arise.

"You will be hunted ... like the rotten hound from Hell you are...and it will be your undoing." He could have sworn the visage of Death had been amused at his remark, the corner of his mouth marked by dark creases.

"I will expect it, and then will I know that *my* time is near."

Jumping back on the ledge he climbed away through the window.

Aside from the near deceased colonel, not one living thing remained. ■

Death Speaks Softly
(Continued from page 11)

Benjamin J. Brewer, first vice president of the Citizens' Bank and Trust Company, dropped open, a cigar tumbled down his vest, and he stared at the back of Henry Pleeber.

Henry took a cab to Mary Seeligson's apartment. She was packing dully. She looked up with red-rimmed eyes when he thrust his head into the room.

"You're leaving?" he said.

She nodded. "I—I couldn't seem to stay here."

"Have you any money?"

She shook her head.

"How would you like to go to California?"

Her eyes widened. "Why—why I'd love to."

"Hitchhike, I mean."

Some of the sadness left her eyes and she laughed softly. "I think that would be wonderful, Henry!"

He gathered her in his arms and much to his amazement, she didn't protest in the slightest. A few minutes later he whispered, "Remind me to introduce you to a friend of mine who's going with us. His name is Jimmy." ■

The Story of
Misión San Juan Capistrano

BY H. BEDFORD-JONES

From the earth they made me,
A grey adobe slab;
By my fellows laid me,
Sun-baked, ugly, drab.
From the dust they called me
Who had been a clod,
Plastered me and walled me —
Set me to serve God!

THE ADOBE

OUT of the south came Junipero Serra the Franciscan, conquering the land with faith, a Cross, and an adobe brick.

California's Via Crucis was mile-stoned with adobes. This was a land all but tree-less; the most natural and easily made material was the sun-baked clay brick. Indeed, it was the only constructive material at the disposal of the first padres.

Misón San Juan Capistrano was founded October 30, 1775. Eight days later came news of the native uprising at San Diego. In all haste Fray Lasuen buried the two mission bells and fled.

In the following year came Padre Serra the Fundator in person, and reestablished the work. He chose a new and better site, between the Trabuco and San Juan creeks, within sight of the sea; and consecrated this foundation November 1, 1776. Then he departed and the work was taken up by his helpers — Padres Mugartégui and Amúrrio.

NO monastery was this place, no secluded spot for meditation and repose; but a school of industrial and manual training where the Indians were taught to know God, and to serve Him in love. Here was preached the mystery of service — to borrow honest Will Comfort's phrase; the mystery of creative labor, of honesty in one's handiwork . The first result of this was the adobe.

Adobe bricks are excellent things in themselves, but they must be protected from the rains. In a country where every scrap of material must be formed from the raw earth-givings, such protection means labor.

The padres labored; their mission was built from adobe and tiles, rawhide and mortar, reeds and boulders.

In the Cañada del Orno, "little canon of the oven," just north of the mission ruins, the remains of the kilns may still be seen. Here were made tiles of many shapes, but all of the same tender red.

Some were square, and these were used to floor the corridors; some were oblong, and these went to build the columns and arches, and to roof them; some were regular roofing tiles, curved and fitted to run water. All may be seen in service to this day.

BEFORE the actual building, all things had to be shown to the guilders. These neophytes, as the Indian converts were termed, learned to use carts and oxen, to make tiles, to transform into cement and mortar the limestone, so laboriously fetched twelve miles over the hills.

Meantime, food had to be" won from the earth and the necessities of life provided. Open ditches and tiled conduits were run from the streams, forming an extensive irrigation system. Gardens, orchards, and vineyards were laid out and the neophytes were shown how to care for them. Each day the advantages of this site chosen by Fray Serra became more evident.

Gradually the adobe walls went up; and, rising, they enclosed workshops. Neophyte carpenters hewed out ceiling-rafters of syc-amore beams, brought from the hills twenty miles away, and carved the quaintly mortised door and window frames. The smithy pro-

H. BEDFORD-JONES (1887-1949) authored over 100 novels. In some circles, he was referred to as the "King of the Pulps". He wrote for several pulp magazines, his main market being *Blue Book*. Bedford-Jones was prominent in the area of historical fiction. He also worked as a journalist for the *Boston Globe*.

"The Misión of San Juan Capistrano" originally appeared in a self-published 1918 pamphlet. *Young Kit Carson*, HBJ's long-lost novel, is now available from Bold Venture Press.

duced nails, locks, hinges and tools.

Less skilled workers brought tules, reeds from the creek-beds, and cut up rawhide. Tules were laid upon the rafters, bound down and made fast with rawhide, and plastered over. In this fashion were made ceilings.

Day by day the dried adobes took higher form, firmer shape; the walls were from two to seven feet thick. The arches rose around a patio of an acre in area, each side being about two hundred feet in length, but no two sides being exactly parallel.

Separated from the arches by a roofed, open corridor were the buildings, running completely around the patio. Not all were erected at once, but there was no haste. All eternity lay ahead for this work.

Were a stone laid, were a bolt set, were a nail driven — it was done for ever. Here was no careless construction , no shoddy work: these men labored not for men, but served God.

Until the adobes returned to dust again this place would endure.

TWENTY years passed. Hugely had the mission prospered. Neophytes, who were now known as San Juaneños, dwelt by the hundred in their own adobe houses, just across the plaza.

Besides the high large church, with its choir-loft and softly tinted walls, there were shops in which were made soap, blankets, candles, sombreros and leather goods.

In the southwest corner was a flat roof for drying fruits. The northeast and north buildings were store-houses for grains, hides, oil and tallow. At the west were the vats and smithy, the oil and wine presses.

From the west front were brought out more arches; an extension of the buildings struck forth into the plaza. Here lay the store-houses, school, and at the end, the quarters and arched bell of the lazy garrison.

Vineyards, orchards and gardens flourished greatly . Thousands of cattle roamed the hills, and the San Juan horses were famous in the land. The mission had outlying rancherias, settlements of San Juaneños who saw to the crops and cattle — and who doubled the talents in their keeping.

No more clay bricks lay baking in the sun.

DURING those twenty years of service and growth, a vision had been in the forming.

All that could be done with adobe, bad been done. Massive walls, arches, all manner of structures — these were finished. But already the padres had begun to look ahead. Not theirs was the ability to rest content with having done enough. Men never do enough for God.

Twenty miles away in the mountains were sycamores. Near the Misón Vieja, Fray Lasuén's old foundation six miles up the canon, was a fine store of sandstone. Twelve miles distant was limestone. At the ocean shore were boulders and sand.

With the close of the year 1796, the padres saw their vision clearly . They began to make diamond-shaped tiles, and sent for a stone-mason .

***

Out of the quarry cut and laid,
Brown hands brought me , unafraid;

Carved me with symbols that had no
   name,
Set me to hold a high arch-frame.
Vanished are they with all their race
Yet here dwell I in my given place;
Washed of the rain, burnt of the sun,
Waiting with God till the years be
   done.

THE KEYSTONE

GOD has given us wealth and workmen and eager hearts. Now let us put our talents to account in His service!

In this spirit the two mission fathers obtained their stone-mason and set to work on a nine-years' contract with God.

On February 2, 1797, the task was begun. This was the Vision a great church all of stone, the grandest house of worship in the Californias . Some of the Baja California churches were marvelous things, carven and dighted with precious gifts; but they were small. This was to be large, beautiful, splendid in its solemnity and grandeur.

They laid it out in the form of a Latin cross, 175 by 80 feet. The walls were to be two yards thick, all of stone and cement; the roof was to be formed by seven bovedas, or domes; the entire building was to be one solid mass of pure masonry .

So the work began.

WEEK after week, month after month, year after year, the purpled hills looked down upon moving files of men, women and children.

Carretas, or ox-carts of two wheels, formed a constant line between the new mission and the Misión Vieja, where lay the sandstone quarries; but not carretas alone. The San Juaneños carried stones on their heads; even the children came bearing stones — twelve miles back and forth, day after day and year after year. Although the neophytes were numbered by the hundreds, the walls were six feet thick.

In the workshops was redoubled toil and labor. The weavers, oil and wine makers, cordwainers, clothiers and candle fashioners must continue work as usual. All regular business must go on, for the mission was self-supporting.

Out in the sun stood the stone-mason with his neophyte pupils, teaching these apprentices the mystery of the keystone, and the carding thereof. The keystones of the tiled arches had been tiles. Now this arch-key took on new meaning and importance.

From the kilns came the tiles, diamond shaped, for the flooring of the new church alone. Month by month up rose the walls, as endless processions wended in, some from the quarries, some from the ocean, othersome from the mountains or limestone cliffs. Concrete was mixed and laid. Slowly the massive walls drew nearer to heaven.

AND the spirit of it all lay in the keystones and lintels, the cornices and capitals. With time, the apprentices became master masons; beneath their hands the rough ashlars were perfected, and in turn these perfect ashlars grew to living jewels of their craft.

For they carded these, not with emblems of the faith, but with strange flowing symbols deeply chiseled and carefully balanced. In those symbols was something of the pagan, something which the good padres assure did not inspire. Perhaps the inspiration came from the quivering sunlight, the rounded hills, the far blue line of the ocean.

The door lintels, carved in conservative cruciform designs, were strikingly different and in their way no less beautiful.

But in the keystones were sermons.

THREE years passed, and the century ended with the work only one-third completed. Still the hundreds of laborers went about their tasks, while the padres planned and directed, yet without neglecting their spiritual trestle-boards.

Gone was the stone-mason, leaving a greater genius than his own with the pupils of his teaching. The bluish grey sandstone still came from the quarry, the carvers still wrought with the slow patience of their race. Neither gaudy nor baroque was their work; they had learned temperance, prudence, fortitude and justice, these entering largely into their labor.

Another three years crept on. Frey Vicente Fuster went the way of all flesh and the vacancy was filed by one Jose Faura. What mattered names ? These men lived for the salvation of souls, and to the glory of God.

Somewhere within the walls rests Brother Vicente, his grave unknown , unmarked; yet his memory is more enduring than bronze.

SLOWLY the great edifice drew upward. The lofty campanile began to rise — up and up, ever climbing skyward, until it could be discerned for ten miles; the sound of its high bells carried even farther.

Other three years passed , but now more swiftly. The floor was laid, the carven doors and windows were placed, the last capital and column were set in their concrete beds, the plaster was drawn over the rough walls, and the stone-chips were cleared from the patio.

Not yet was the task completed, however. Remained some delicate gilding and tinting with soft ochres and the tender sheen of copper-ground ship's paint. The dull colorings blended most exquisitely wifh the deep red of the tiles, the creamy white of the plaster, until the high-towering transept and sanctuary Wre gorgeous in soft harmony. It was finished.

NOW came a splendid and notable company wending unto the Misión San Juan Capistrano.

Came Don Jose Juaquin de Arrellaga, bringing his officers and soldiers from all the presidios; he was governor of the province and a very worthy gentleman. Came Fray Estevan Tapis, president of the missions. Came many brethren of the Order from their scattered posts: San Gabriel Archangel, San Luis Rey de Francia, Santa Barbara, and others. Came neophytes from the neighbor missions, with Spaniards and half breeds, in great numbers.

To receive them were the builders, the San Juaneños; and Padres Faura and Santiago, whose labors had brought to completion this work.

Thus at last was the great edifice consecrated ; and, save to the Supreme Architect, there was no church debt.

***

Unto the sky
Tower we afar,
Calling on high,
Calling men nigh —
Nigh unto prayer.
Over the worn
Desert-land's glare,
To sundrift and star
Our call is upborne,
"Come ye to prayer!"
Ever we cry,
Never we cease,
"Come ye to prayer,
 Here is God's peace!"

THE HIGH BELLS

VITALLY important to the work of the mission, and symbolic to Indian hearts of all for which the mission stood, were its bells.

The daily regime, in fact the entire mission life, was under the regulation of the bells. Meals, worship, labor — for each occupation of brethren and neophytes the bells were struck. Was not each act a service of God?

Today, those bells, four in number, hang in a low wall; the largest is dated 1796, and its inscription is in honor of Padres Fuster and Santiago. Next in size is that holding a bold proclamation: "Ruelas made me, and my name is San Juan, 1796."

Who was this Ruelas? We do not know. The one man who left his name graven upon this structure, he alone has been totally forgotten.

These two bells may have been recast from those buried in 1775 by) Padre Lasuén; but according to local traditions the buried bells were never found.

Dated "San Antonio, 1804" and "San Rafael, 1804," the two smaller bells that hang here were evidently sent from other missions to enrich the campanile of the great new church.

HARSH and strident, the bells rang afar, clanging birth and marriage, sorrow and toil, worship and death. So high stood the campanile that it could be seen from Los Alisos, ten miles distant. And for six years the high bells swung there, until the Master's hand touched upon them.

The builders of the church departed, and in their places walked Padres Francisco Suner and Josef Barona — men sent hither to meet heart-rending ferial days, and one of them destined to suffer at the hands of evil men.

December 8, 1812, came and went again. For us who look back upon a vanished era, it is a day of questioning.

It was the feast of the Immaculate Conception.

THE first mass was for adults; thus, no children were in the church. Why? Was this by chance?

The service began. The tongues of the bells were replaced by chanting; the Indian flutists, drummers and violinists lifted the voices into resounding cadences; Vancouver's barrel-organ-piped throatily.

Candles blazed; at the altar was the padre, wearing the white-and-gold chasuble which had come from Mexico City. Wrought by pious hands, sent to some older mission, it had been outworn and replaced and sent on, at last reaching San Juan, still stiff and gorgeous. And it is there now.

The offertory was finished. In the campanile two boys were ringing the bells for second mass, bronze tongues were clanging, clanging — why should it have befallen at that instant?

For of a sudden the vaulted domes were rent asunder.

WITH the wave-like motion of the walls, the doors jammed; above, the roof cracked open to the blue sky). Although the celebrant motioned the people toward the sacristy) door, not all could obey) .

From above came a rush of rubble as the walls were ripped asunder and the domes fell. Dust-darkness, shrieks .... chaos. And then one tremendous crash that drowned all else; the proud campanile had fallen!

Instead of burying all beneath its ruins, it fell away from the church , out into the plaza. Why?

AFTER two days of searching and labor, forty bodies were recovered; others were not recovered. The padres buried the dead, whose names may) to this day) be read in the records.

Nine years in building, the church had served God six years when it was shattered. The sanctuary and transept alone were unruined, unharmed, left intact. Why ?

Other structures suffered little; the padres took up the daily round anew, not trying to rebuild. In after times such efforts were made, but came to naught. Again the mission prospered, dealt largely in hides and grain and cattle; perhaps the brethren cherished ambitions, yet in the days of

prosperity that followed the earthquake, the church was not rebuilt. Why?

These queries we cannot answer.

***

All the night is deep and still;
Coyote, do you hear the thunder
	groveling?
Stars fling silver over the hill
Where the gaunt grey beast is
	prowling,
Up at the star-flecked night-sky
	howling,
While men Watch not but sleep their
	fill —
Oye , oye !
When the dawn comes grey
Coyote, do you hear the thunder
	growling?

THE COYOTE

AFTER these things fell evil days upon the place , and yet more evil men.

Always had Mexico eyed greedily the rich Alta California missions, posting soldiers at each one and claiming civil authority. The cholo soldiers did as they pleased, defying the padres, and at San Juan they most grievously maltreated Padre Barona.

Also, these cholos brought vices and drunkeness among the Indians; no good thing came out of Mexico. The neophytes were thrown into the hands of the flesh and the devil. Simple souls were they, not hard to lead astray; the olden days were gone, and into their world had come greed.

IN 1833 the missions were finally seized , and San Juan Capistrano was the first to suffer.

The San Juaneños saw the rule pass into new hands; they saw the lands sold off; they saw men casting lots for the sacred Vestments; they) saw the mission buildings desecrated, and themselves cast adrift.

Later came smallpox and dwelt with them, so that the San Juaneños perished as a people.

Now the coyote comes into the story. Among the Indians was a saying, part of a folk-tale not yet lost: "*Oye los truenos, coyote?*" Dost hear the thunder, coyote? There is pith in the words.

After many years were the mission buildings, their contents partially intact, restored to their church, through the work of Dona Ysadora Pico de Forster. It was too late to save the neophytes but it was not too late to save the buildings; however, the place was forgotten of the world . Yet what matter whether the world remembers?

Years fled, twenty or more. Services were held occasionally. Looters found the place rich; but their hands took amazingly little.

Here were statues, wrought from Spanish woods and decked with gold. Silver candlesticks, torches, crosses and other objects of metal were not lacking. Also, rare paintings and broideries.

SOMEHOW, down the years, the mission held these things unwarded, unlocked. The adobe buildings around the patio crumbled; earth hid the tender red tiles; men quarried materials from the ruins for their own uses. Coyotes howled in the desolate patio; this was the final requiem.

But those remaining of the San Juaneños whispered: "*Oye los truenos, coyote?*"

The words held significance; not often is thunder heard hereabouts, and a thunderstorm is rare indeed. Perhaps — who knows? — to the Indian mind it typified the voice and action of Deity. But the coyote, like the temple looter, was the most despicable of all things. "Dost hear the thunder, coyote?" The saying lingered.

Within the mission were desolation and graves, ruin and sadness, neglect and emptiness. Yet, from time to time, God thundered upon the hills.

God does not forget. He was raising up a man to His work.

***

He heard a solemn anthem swim
Upon the swallows' twittered cries;
The bare brown hills became to him
A skimmer of sun-symphonies;
Athwart the crumbling cloister-shade
An angel's wing limned lanes of
        light,
And from forgotten graves out-
        strayed
Low whisperings upon the night.
With adze and plane and rugged
        beam
He fell to hewing out his dream.

THE MAN

A MAN came to San Juan to die. Smitten by the white plague, he was denied all hope. Since he had but to await death, yet wished to remain in the Divine service, he was sent to the abode of desolation.

I do not think it occurred to the Man,

or to anyone else, that all his life had been shapen toward his coming here to die. God never makes mistakes .

The Man, burning with a deep spirituality, came here to die. Only forgotten graves awaited him; only the work of the Landmarks Club had saved the mission from total destruction.

Weeds grew, shoulder-high in the holy places. Tourists defaced every wall. With each rain, more of the ruins vanished. The tinted chancel-dome of the high church was covered with swallows' mud nests. The graves of the padres were lost.

THE Man lived among the cholos. Each day, expecting death, he visited the ruins and cleared a space; he uncovered the beautiful tiles, such as remained. At every turn he found wonderful things: fragments of carved work, bits of iron lovingly wrought in the mission forge, scraps of materials rarely worked. All these he saved.

He drew close to the folk, learned their speech, won their love. They told him ancient legends, folklore, bits of mission history no one else could have gleaned. And still God thundered upon the hills.

To his surprise the Man did not die. Slowly, as he worked amid the ruins, strength returned to him. The mystery of service now brought him its unsought reward — a vision.

Ruined, despoiled, the old mission endured above those who had laid it low. In itself it was a Vision; only where there is no vision do the people perish. The Man beheld here a life-work; because he had this vision he did not perish but took up the task.

Through what doubt and despair he struggled, none other can know. Often his Vision seemed destroyed, as difficulties loomed larger. Each forward step seemed to attain new troubles.

But God never makes mistakes. Every scrap of material found, with legend and story to guide him, the Man set to work. Other missions had been "restored," slathered with plaster, brick and glass, painted in terrible fervor. But to this task God had sent no restorer. He had sent an artist.

NOW the Man dwelt amid the ruins and became the Padre both in fact and spirit. He, too, hewed sycamore beams for rafters; he, too, carved and mortised his window-frames, after the fashion of those remaining. When he drove a nail, it was a nail made in the forge.

Among the ruins were scraps of old frescoes. Artists visiting the place saw the Padre's vision. In the rooms he restored they copied the old work, line for line, color for color; not in the ecstasy of creation but in the loving care of service.

The Padre bought new brick and tile. He traded new for old, collecting from the town and ranches much that was valuable in his vision. All such things furthered his labors.

WHENCE came the money for this work? From both ecclesiastical and private sources; let us say, from God.

No hire could buy such labor as the Padre gave to his Vision, for his remuneration was not of the earth . Before him lay eternity for this task, and there was no haste. If he laid but one tile each day, and laid it well, he was content.

It was this spirit which made the old world's wonders, and makes the new world wonder. It is rarely found in this country. Once it was here, indeed, but with the displacement of thoroughness by greed, as a standard of craftmanship, it vanished. This spirit made the rugs of Persia, the Flemish buildings, the bronze-craft of China, the illuminations which Irish monks taught the schoolmen of Europe. Rugs, buildings, bronzes, illuminations — these are made no more in the old spirit; they are made but to perish, for their makers have no vision. But at San Juan Capistrano the spirit lingers.

***

FOR years the mission was desolate and abandoned, visionless. Its people perished and vandals held it at their mercy. Yet the spirit of the padres abode in the place where had served; then came the Padre. In him the old spirit revived, and the ancient vision. Every stone and carving and crumbling fresco cried out to him; Adobe and Keystone and Bell carried to him their message.

Under the spell of his Vision, ruin and destruction evolved into beauty and service. Nor did he serve the dead only, for children sat at his feet and learned. His was the legacy of human fragments in the despised cholo, the halfbreed, the Mexican and Indian.

With such fragments he builded . In him they saw, not the alien, but the Padre whose soul housed veneration and deep kindliness, and a vision. They answered to the vision of their fathers.

The townfolk jeered because he traded new bricks for old, made nails in the forge, left his new doors bare until he could get the paint used by the padres. As the fragments, human and divine, upgrew beneath his hand, the scoffling ceased.

***

AND today the old place is alive. It is alive with its ancient beauty, alive with graves and ruins, alive with its rebirth. Its people are not perishing but are thriving. Tourist vandals have been turned into paying guests.

Never will the mission be restored to its pristine grandeur; and it is better so. No longer are neophytes at hand to work in shop and field, no longer do its cattle roam the hills, no longer does the land need it as a center of industry and agriculture. The land needs it only as the house of God . Each crumbled arch, each delicate keystone, bears a spiritual message.

SAN Juan does not lack relics of more material interest — Padre Serra's book of the dead, a letter writ by Fray Crespi before San Diego was founded, ancient silver and vessels and paintings.

The Padre, too, has great store of tales and legends drawn from the hearts of his people; and these he will someday , perhaps, make into a book.

He will do so — five, ten, twenty years hence. Why hurry? Who serves God, not man, finds a calm poise in life; to each day some task, but God sets the pace.

Perhaps this, after all, is the greatest lesson.   ∎

Reign of Terror

(Continued from page 49)

You needed something to solve, so I gave that to you." He looked down at my hand in my pocket. My knuckles were white around the pistol. "Now here we are."

"Why not do it yourself?"

He turned towards the lake. "Everyday I come to this spot and try to convince myself to walk in until I reach the bottom. I can't. The act would betray my innermost sensibilities. To do so would be to admit defeat." He turned back. "This is now your role in our arrangement."

I sneered. "I'm a lawyer, pal, not a killer. I pay the bills convincing people I'm right, not shooting 'em dead."

"You're clever enough to know I didn't bring you here for legal advice, but you're here anyways." He took a breath. "One of us is leaving here in a bag. The choice is up to you."

The gun hung heavy at my side and a cold bead of sweat found its way down my brow. He started to approach. After a few steps, I raised the pistol. Then he came at me quick. As soon as he was close enough for me to see the pupils in his deep, sad eyes, time stopped.

I pulled the trigger twice, which slowed him down. Two more stopped him. Each shot pierced through the night, its echo a deafening reminder of all the violence that even the tranquility of the setting couldn't quell. He crumbled to his side, quivered for a moment, and then died. I was getting used to being around corpses. I put the pistol back in my overcoat. I took out the big bills he gave me when I first met him, crumbled them into a ball, and tossed them into the lake. Then I enjoyed the calm of the aftermath for a few moments before finding a payphone to call the cops.

After I filled my client with lead and called it in, you bet the police had plenty of questions. Anything I was willing to answer I answered truthfully, and the rest I told them to arrest me or shove off. They told me not to leave town and that I'd be hearing from them and other nonsense cop talk they probably learned at the pictures.

Lucky for my client, I was bound to keep his confidential disclosures under my hat even after his death. But maybe this time I'd need to spill to save my own hide. Things would get sticky the next few months. Good thing I knew where to find a decent lawyer.

That night I ordered pork chops at Ben's with all the trimmings, and Old Forester with a cube in it. I didn't think much about what the DA was going to do with me, and I didn't think much about how I'd given a killer everything he wanted.

Instead, I thought about how my client would be the last dead body in Golden Gate Park for a while. ∎

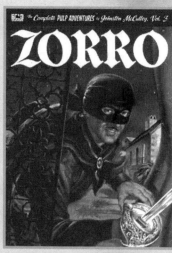

ZORRO.
The Complete Pulp Adventures by Johnston McCulley

The Curse of Capistrano's original adventures —
collected for the first time in paperback and hardcover.

www.boldventuepress.com

Made in the USA
Las Vegas, NV
04 December 2020